The Bayshire

T.S.O. Book 2

R.E. Klinzing

Published by: Bayshire Publications
Cover design by R.E. Klinzing

ISBN: 978-1-7373043-0-2

reklinzing.com

For my sister Audrey. Thanks for being my wall. ☺

The Bayshire

Chapter 1
Meeting the Boss

He came at me, running across the mat. I ducked my head to avoid his blow as I spun around to face him from behind. I kicked him square in the back, pushing him forward.

"Better luck next time, pal," I said, spinning around as I wiped the sweat from my brow. I took a step forward, and he grabbed me from behind. He wrapped his arms around me and took me down in a tackle, leaving me on my stomach. "Ow." I rolled over onto my back, grabbing at my stomach. "Really?" I groaned at Miles. His skin was glistening with sweat, his black hair a complete mess.

"You need to watch your back, Agent Mills. Unless your opponent is detained or stops breathing, they can always turn on you."

Of course, I already knew that. I understood that better than a lot of agents at the T.S.O. I was the best combat field operative in Ohio. "You're too melodramatic, Miles." I pulled myself to my feet.

"You make yourself too vulnerable." Miles grabbed a water bottle from the side of the mat. "You're a good fighter, Alexis. Your mind's just not in the right place today."

Well, of course I was distracted right now. The T.S.O. offered me the position of a lifetime only a few weeks ago. "You do things your way, and I'll do them mine," I said, smiling at him as I fixed my gloves. Miles, AKA Agent Darwin, loved to have me question my way of things. He was definitely a "by the book" type of guy. And I was most definitely not. Miles was seventeen, but liked to act like he was much older. We had these hand-to-hand combat practice sessions once a week, just to stay on our toes.

"I still don't know why they chose you as the Defense Tactics Instructor," Miles said, taking off his gloves.

"Because they know a good fighter when they see one." I felt like I was walking on air. A few weeks ago, the board of directors selected me as this year's Defense Tactics Instructor for first year campers at the T.S.O. Training Camp. I was only sixteen. It was rare a teenage operative was selected as an instructor, but I had been practicing hand-to-hand combat since I was ten. It was one reason they recruited me. They named the Teen Spy Organization after its never-ending goal of having teenagers in the field, but adults still ran it. It was a major honor to be a camp instructor. It was the type of job I had wanted since I realized it was a position. My job would be to teach new agents how to fight and protect themselves. I wanted the job because of my sister, Hailey.

"Same time next week?" Miles asked.

I nodded, grabbed my backpack, and headed for the door. I had a meeting with the Director, which could only mean one thing. A new case, a new mission, a new chance to kick someone's butt. I couldn't wait to find out what it was. Tracking down a major criminal? Rescuing someone who was in trouble? Stopping a predicted crime? The possibilities seemed endless.

My mind raced, my palms were sweaty from my workout, and my heart pounded as I left the gym through the opened doors.

"Good luck!" Miles shouted after me.

"Don't need luck!"

Entering Mr. Martial's office, the figure standing in the corner made me regret stepping inside. Only Agent Watson had the nerve to glare at me that way. I could feel his presence in every ounce of my being. Agent Watson was the only agent here at the Ohio T.S.O. base that I couldn't stand since the day I met him at camp. *Don't think about him*, I told myself, dismissing him from my mind. *I need to focus on the task at hand, Mr. Martial's new assignment.*

"Yes, Director?" I asked, putting on a straight face. I tugged at my fingerless gloves. I had been waiting for a fresh case for a while. It was about time.

"You're being assigned a new case," Mr. Martial responded. Mr. Martial was an interesting man. He didn't like anyone. He was hard on everybody, but seemed to especially pick on the experienced agents like myself. His dark brown skin and black hair complemented his dark brown eyes, the eyes that always seemed to see right through me.

"Why is Agent Watson here?" I asked, watching him smirk at me from his place against the wall. His green eyes studied me. His military buzz cut only annoyed me more. I shifted my weight from foot to foot.

"Don't mind me," Agent Watson said. "Just here to watch the show."

"Whatever." I turned my attention to Mr. Martial and the reason I was in his office. "Mr. Martial, what's the case?"

"Agent Mills," Mr. Martial started, "There is a stone. The Bayshire Stone. It was discovered on an archeological dig and is being held here in Ohio in the hands of a private investor. Agent Mills, this stone is very dangerous. You need to retrieve it immediately."

"Where is it located?" I asked, tucking a loose strand of hair behind my ear.

"It is currently in the possession of an investor known as Mr. Randall Bard. This man was in charge of the dig site when the Bayshire was discovered. The Bayshire has been marked dangerous since it caused an explosion during its first phases of observation and testing. Mr. Bard is in charge of the stone, but we have decided that his care for it and continuous pulic display of it is too dangerous. Randall Bard has a history of criminal activity even though there isn't anything on public record. And his need for public power has led us to believe he may misuse the stone."

"Why isn't it a job for the police?" I asked.

"Because as far as they are concerned he never did anything wrong. Agent Mills, this man has used his wealth to buy himself out of trouble before, and he will do it again. But the Bayshire is too dangerous, and public safety has to be taken into consideration here. It must be retrieved by the T.S.O. You can pick a small team of agents to go with you and retrieve the stone from his house."

"Okay, Boss. When do you want me to leave?" I glanced behind me at Watson. "Is this a case for both of us?" I asked. "You know that's a bad idea."

Mr. Martial, his hands holding himself up against his desk, finally said what I was hoping to hear. "No, this is not Watson's case. Agent Watson, we're done here, thank you." Agent Watson sighed in annoyance and left the room, slamming the door behind him. "As I was saying," Mr. Martial snapped at me, "You and your team will go after him tomorrow at 0730 hours. Here is Randall Bard's schedule, his address, home layout, and the records we have on the Bayshire." Mr. Martial handed me a file. "You will also need these." The Director handed me a black backpack and a pair of gloves. "We don't know how hazardous the stone is to human contact, so use these as a precaution."

"Yes, Sir." I studied the gloves before putting them and the file into the backpack. The gloves were black, with a special padding on the palms and the fingers. The backpack was lined with something that felt almost rubbery.

"And, Agent Mills?" I met Mr. Martial's gaze.

"Yes?"

"You're supposed to be the Defense Tactics Instructor. People are expecting the best out of you. Don't mess this up for yourself."

I nodded. "I won't. I promise."

"You're dismissed."

I turned the corner that would take me back to the elevator and the coffee shop on the street level four stories above the T.S.O. base. As I flipped through the file, my mind flickered over what I needed to do for my cover job at the coffee shop. It really was ingenious. What kid didn't have a part-time job? Mine was just a cover for the T.S.O. at the main entrance to the Ohio T.S.O. base. The coffee shop was as ordinary as any other coffee shop in the country, unless you entered the back room and found the hidden hand scanner. Of course, it wouldn't do anything unless it recognized your handprint. The coffee shop was located right above the base, and was one of the main access points in the city. I stepped onto the elevator platform and waited for the slab of concrete under me to move.

The elevator carried me up four stories with a quiet whoosh.

The elevator landed and the silver doors opened. In front of them was a simple door. I turned the handle, and it

5

opened into the back supply room of the coffee shop. It was small and cluttered. The door shut and clicked behind me, sealing off the entrance to the T.S.O. The space was filled with rows of shelves stocked with food items and extra disposable cups and dishes. I walked through the shelves. The small freezer was through the door on my left, and the office/empty break room on my right. I headed straight for the front of the café.

"What's the mission?"

I turned to face my partner, Agent B. Technically, his name was Tanner. I smiled up at him as he approached from the front of the shop. Don't let his tall, muscular features distract you. He was as fit as a horse, his toned arms crossed in front of his chest as he stood in front of me. He looked silly in the white apron. His blue eyes looked down at me, and I resisted the urge to smile.

Unlike Miles, Tanner was quiet, reserved, and caring. The guy wouldn't hurt a fly unless it was, you know, an enemy of the state or something. And I trusted him with my life.

"We have to retrieve a dangerous rock. I'm going to do more research about it tonight before we leave tomorrow."

"Are we going undercover?" Tanner asked, pulling the apron over his head.

"Of course we're going undercover. Have you met me?"

"Hilarious." His lips tugged slightly with a smile. It was that discreet. "Who are we taking?"

"What about Allison and Daniel? They could use the field training."

"Sounds good."

"I'll send you the details tonight."

"Looking forward to it." I looked up at him and smiled, taking in his heartwarming gaze. He couldn't be more perfect. As a partner, of course.

Chapter 2
No School Tomorrow

I flipped on the light switch and took a seat at my desk. The file Mr. Martial gave me about the case had been thicker than I expected. I laid out the papers on my desk and turned on my music, the sound of rock music filling my bedroom. My parents didn't exactly agree with the music I enjoyed, but I wouldn't listen to anything else. It kept my adrenaline pumping.

According to Randall Bard's files, he was a very distinguished man. He lived in a penthouse on the top floor of an apartment building in the middle of the city. He collected various artifacts from all over the world and often loaned them to various museums. I could see why the public's safety could be at stake. How he ever managed to get permission to have the Bayshire out in public, I have no idea.

The Bayshire Stone was more interesting than I thought it would be, for a rock anyway. I pulled out a photo of it and tried to memorize what it looked like. The stone was the shape of a misshapen oval, only four inches in height and seven inches in width. It was a tint of red and somewhat transparent. Inside there appeared to be the shape of an X.

Why is it so important? I kept reading, wondering what exactly made this stone so dangerous.

The Bayshire Stone comprises multiple elements with high electrical conductivity. The molecular structure within the stone is rare, creating an extremely dangerous energy field.

The Bayshire Stone, when exposed to the right frequency, is prone to cause severe electrical hazards. It can absorb energy, therefore causing major blackouts, and release dangerously high levels of electricity at one time, resulting in electromagnetic waves.

"Okay," I murmured to myself, "You have to confiscate an electrically unstable rock. A rock that acts like it has magical powers. No problem."

"Alexis?" Mom peeked through the door.

"Yes, Mom?" I placed my hand over the top of the papers.

"Dinner's ready. What are you working on?" She asked.

"Just some homework."

"Alright. Come down soon." Mom closed the door, and I listened as the sound of her footsteps quieted down the hallway.

"Sorry, no school tomorrow," I whispered to myself, putting all the papers back in the folder. School only had about a week left anyway, and I had already completed most of my finals.

I attended a private school around the corner from the coffee shop/T.S.O. entrance. The T.S.O. would give my school a note saying that I was out sick. This wasn't the first time I skipped school for "educational purposes" with a note from my parents or doctor to explain my absence. The T.S.O.

must have forged a lot of doctor's notes for agents, but no one seemed to notice. Besides, going undercover and breaking into a penthouse to steal a powerful stone seemed much more exciting than listening to Sarah, my best friend, take up my whole lunch break talking about her science teacher's latest fail at an experiment.

I slipped the file into my bag alongside the gloves. A new mission. Tomorrow was too far away.

Chapter 3
Retrieving a Dangerous Rock

"Randall Bard lives on the top floor of the penthouse," I said, excitement tenting my voice as I spoke. I wasn't taking down a notorious criminal, but at least I got to see a penthouse. In the three years of being a secret agent, I had yet to go undercover in some rich guy's house. This job was full of surprises.

"What's the plan, Agent Mills?" Allison asked. She and Daniel were both in advanced training, shadowing agents, like myself, in the field.

"We'll be going undercover." I looked down at the floor plan laid out across the desk. We all hovered around a table in the T.S.O. base's cafeteria. Few people were here this early in the morning. "Randall Bard has the building's cleaning crew come in twice a week, so that will be our way in. The plan is to get in and out before the real cleaning crew actually arrives.

"Allison and Daniel, you guys will stand guard in the hallway. There's usually a cleaning crew there anyway, so you'll blend in perfectly. If you hear or see anything, you alert us immediately." I instructed them on how to contact us through our phones.

"And us?" Tanner asked.

"We'll go inside and retrieve the Bayshire Stone. I'll need you to deactivate his security system."

"Copy that."

"Here are your uniforms. We leave in five minutes."

After putting on my uniform, I met everyone else in the back room of the coffee shop. The uniform was a button-down shirt with a collar and black pants, pretty fancy for a house cleaning uniform. We had created them to match the uniforms from the cleaning crews that worked the apartment. My arms felt bare without my leather jacket.

"Alright, let's go." We all piled into one of the T.S.O. issued vehicles, Tanner in the driver's seat. I seriously wanted to be the one driving. But no, my parents still wouldn't allow me to start Driver's Ed despite turning sixteen months ago. So my partner had to drive on my mission. I went over the floor plans again.

We arrived at the building and entered the lobby. I pushed the button on the service elevator and we stepped inside. Allison manned the cleaning cart. We were going to break into someone's private home. There was a tugging in my gut telling me I couldn't do this. Thoughts of my sister flashed through my mind and I pushed them away. I needed to focus on the here and now, not the past. This was different. I looked over at Tanner, who smiled back at me. Immediately, I felt better. This was going to be exciting. The elevator started moving.

When the elevator door opened, we rushed into the hallway. After turning a corner, we stood face to face with Mr. Bard. My breath caught in my throat. He hardly looked at us. A clean-cut shave and hair slicked back with gel that was probably expensive. The smell of his cologne invaded my senses, and I resisted the urge to cough.

"Excuse me," I said, moving out of his way. He said nothing to me, just looked down at his phone and walked down the hall. We stood there for a moment. I peeked around the corner in time to see the elevator doors close behind him.

"That was close," Daniel whispered.

"Okay," I said, ignoring his comment. "You guys stay around here." The two trainees headed down the hall with the cleaning cart. Tanner and I walked down the hall until we arrived at Mr. Bard's front door.

I pulled out one of my favorite gadgets from my pocket. A key card. I scanned the lock with the fake credit card, and it folded itself into the proper type of key to fit into the door lock.

My hands shook as I inserted the key into the lock. I had never broken into a person's house. I told myself I was doing the right thing. No one was going to get hurt. This had to work. I let out a steady breath as I heard it click. "We're in," I whispered.

Tanner pulled a device from his pants pocket and went to work with the security system. I watched his fingers move and tried to slow my heart rate. "Got it," he said.

I opened the door, and we stepped inside.

Chapter 4
Inside a Penthouse

The living room was enormous. I stood in the doorway, taking in the scenery. The walls were white, along with most of the furniture. The wood floors looked spotless, and the view from the windows let us see past his balcony and into the city. A girl could feel like a princess in a place like this. It wasn't my style.

I stepped into the middle of the living room, staying off the white rug. Based on the blueprints, the hallway to my left led to a bedroom, an office, and then a gym. The hall to my right led to the kitchen, bathroom, and master bedroom.

"Where do you think the Bayshire is?" Tanner asked.

"Not in plain sight," I said. Tanner took out a phone, pulled up an app issued by the T.S.O. that would pick up any electromagnetic waves. I had no idea how any of it worked. Leave it to Tanner to handle the technical stuff. "Detecting high energy levels coming from what looks like his bedroom closet. Alexis, that has to be it."

"Let's find out," I said.

I peeked inside the kitchen as we walked down the hall to the master bedroom. The table inside the kitchen was huge. I hurried off before getting too curious about what was in his fridge. Once inside the bedroom, I struggled to relax. We were so close. There was a gigantic bed, a table, and even a couch in the room. It was spotless, unlike mine. The right side of the room had two doors. One led to the bathroom and closet, the other to the outdoor balcony and pool. We walked through the bathroom, and I peeked inside the walk-in closet. It was crazy large. Racks filled with suits, shoes laid out on the floor, a row of ties, a dresser. But no Bayshire Stone.

"I see nothing," Tanner said, peeking his head in through the doorway.

"Me either." I was expecting a safe or something holding the Bayshire. Tanner took a step forward. "Wait!" I shouted.

He froze, looking back at me. "What?"

"Look." I pointed to the corner of the closet above the door. A security camera. Based on the angle of the camera, it was recording the inside of the closet, not the door. Another step and we would have been seen.

"I shut them down though," Tanner said, looking down at his phone. "Hold on. It's on a different system. Give me a second." Tanner messed with his device. "That should do it. The camera is deactivated." I nodded.

I followed Tanner into the closet. He looked at the camera and nodded his approval. We looked behind the rows of suits and inside the dresser drawers. No stone.

"This doesn't make sense," Tanner said, shaking his head and looking at his phone. "It's got to be right here. The readings are off the charts."

"Let me see that."

Tanner handed me his phone, and I looked at the readings. He was right. Something was definitely here, and it was electrically unstable. I handed back the device, and Tanner started pushing buttons.

"Maybe the readings are wrong, Alexis," he said. Based on his tone, he didn't believe what he was saying.

"No, they were right." I looked at the security camera and followed the direction it was pointing. The dresser. The camera was fixed on the dresser. I studied it, but saw nothing out of place. It was just a dresser. There were two pairs of shoes on top of it, four drawers. Something behind them caught my eye. I pushed the shoes aside.

Bam! "It's right here." The wall was different behind the dresser. There was a line, like a crack in the wallpaper. "Help me move this."

Tanner pocketed his phone, and we pulled the dresser away from the wall. The line reached all the way to the floor, creating a square about the size of the dresser. "Okay, how do we open it? There's got to be a button, or a lever, or something."

I ran my hand along the crease.

"Found it," Tanner said

"Where?" Somehow, he had removed the light switch from the wall. The white square slid upward out of place and uncovered a small button. "Awesome," I whispered. Tanner pushed the button and the square of wall in front of me slid away. Behind it was a safe.

I went down on one knee to figure out how to get in, and Tanner kneeled beside me. I moved over to let him reach the safe. He pulled out yet another device from inside his housekeeping uniform. I watched while Tanner connected his device to the pad on the safe. "That should do it," he whispered. I realized I was staring at him and turned away. After hearing a faint click, he turned the handle and the safe door opened.

There it was. The Bayshire Stone, the thing so dangerous it needed to be locked away by a secret underground organization. "Nice job." Dawning the pair of gloves from Mr. Martial, I reached inside the safe. The red stone was beautiful. It was dangerous. And my job was almost done.

Just as I picked up the stone, a bell chimed on my phone. The warning signal from the agents out in the hall. Tanner put his hand on my shoulder. "We need to go."

I picked up the stone and placed it inside my backpack. Tanner hit the button on the wall and the panel slid shut, hiding the safe. We pushed the dresser back in place, and I placed the shoes on top.

My phone chimed again. I pulled my arms through the backpack straps.

We heard the front door open.

Tanner and I ran out of the closet and back into the bedroom. Footsteps were coming down the hallway.

"Alexis, this way." Tanner waved towards the door to the balcony. He slid it open, and we rushed outside.

I skidded to a stop before plummeting into Randall Bard's private pool on his terrace. We raced around the side of the house, no time to admire the city from so high up. On the other side of the balcony, we could see the living room and dining room through the windows. There was another sliding door that led inside to the living room. It was unlocked.

We stepped inside.

"Come on," I whispered. Before we made it past the couch, a security guard ran through the hall, almost colliding with me. He stopped in front of us, blocking our only exit. Randall Bard came racing out of the hallway, furious.

"Hi," I started. "We're the new cleaning crew."

"I don't have a new cleaning crew," Mr. Bard growled.

"Then we'll just get out of your hair."

17

The security guard ran towards us. Tanner jumped out of his path, grabbed his arm from behind, and pushed him to the ground.

Another man dressed in the same security uniform burst through the door. As he came running for me, I remembered the move Miles used on me yesterday during our one-on-one training. Tanner reached the door. I spun around. Once the security guard was in reach, I wrapped my arms around him, stuck my foot out beside him, and thrust my hips. He flipped over, groaning in pain.

"Are you kidding me?" the investor exclaimed. "Do something!"

I laughed and ran out the door. Allison and Daniel raced toward us down the hall.

"I need backup!" Someone shouted from behind me.

I yelled, waving my arm in the air for Daniel and Allison to turn back around, away from the guards. We crammed into the elevator.

"That was close," Allison said as the elevator slowly took us to the first floor.

"That was kind of fun," I said between breaths. Tanner tilted his head, showing his silent agreement. I handed the backpack to Tanner. But we weren't done yet.

My heart wouldn't calm down from the rush of adrenaline. My fingers were tingling.

"Let's do that again sometime," Daniel said, letting out a deep breath. He was shaking. Of course, he only had two months of fieldwork under his belt.

The elevator doors opened.

And my heart dropped.

Chapter 5
Fight in the Lobby

The fight wasn't over yet. The lobby had to be filled with at least twenty guards. "Do it again, as in right now?" Allison asked.

I forced my blood to pump again, and adrenaline raced through my veins.

"They know we're the good guys, right?" Daniel asked.

I smirked. "Nope." I ran out of the elevator, charging toward the group of security guards. My legs burned as I jumped into motion. This was my favorite part, the fight. Allison ran up beside me. "We are the good guys!" Daniel shouted from behind. I smiled wider at his remark, my cheeks burning.

The first security guard came at us. Allison and I grabbed his arms and pulled him backwards off his feet. Allison turned, elbowing another in the chest. I ran forward, sliding on the floor. The two people in front of me ran into each other as I slid between them.

On my right, five security guards surrounded Tanner. The backpack was in his hands. A woman charged at him. We made eye contact. Tanner threw the backpack into the air. Running a few steps forward, I grabbed the bag and headed for the front entrance.

Someone grabbed my arm. I turned around, confronted by a female guard. She smiled at me. "What do you have there?" she asked.

"Just some homework." Holding the bag in my left arm, I swung myself around and kicked her in the knee before she could throw a punch. She crumpled to her knees. Slipping the backpack over my shoulder, I glanced around the room. Allison and Tanner were working as a team. Three guards lay at their feet. But Daniel? Daniel was in a sticky spot.

"What do I do?" Daniel asked, looking up at me. A security guard was holding him from behind.

"Think!" I shouted. Daniel thought for a moment, then brought his foot up, slamming it down on the security guard's boot. Losing his grip for a moment, Daniel pulled away. He performed a right uppercut, knocking the guard's head backward. I gave him a thumbs up.

Someone hit me in the back. I regained my balance, turning around in time to avoid a blow. I threw a punch, but my opponent blocked it. He grabbed my right arm. I pulled away but didn't escape his swing.

Metal stung my cheek. Following the man's hand as it moved past my face, I saw a brass knuckle ring on his fingers. That's not something a security guard or officer would be wearing. This must be Randall Bard's personal security detail, not a bunch of rent-a-cops. With anger bubbling up inside me, I recoiled and kicked him in the stomach, knocking the air out of him. I knocked his legs out from under him, sending him to the floor.

Placing a finger on my cheek, a warm sticky fluid covered my finger. Blood. Okay, now I was angry.

I spun around, my eyes stopping on a row of seats at the opposite side of the lobby. Two little girls were sitting there, staring at me in terror. My heart stopped. Hailey, my older sister, flashed in my mind. The horrific memory made my entire body shudder. I ran to the girls and kneeled in front of them. I couldn't let these girls get hurt. "It'll be alright," I said. "Get out of here." They dashed out the door, holding onto each other. My face burned with anger, blood dripping from my cheek. Hopefully, they didn't get hurt.

I fought to regain my composure. Still kneeling on the floor, a guard charged for me. There was a low coffee table in front of me, and I saw my chance open up. The security officer ran in my direction and jumped onto the table. Just as his feet hit the surface, I rolled under the table, safely coming out the other side as he landed on the opposite side, the backpack still strapped over my shoulders.

I glared at the man. It was the same security guard from upstairs. I saw Tanner lying on the floor. He sat up, but the motion looked painful. Four guards held Allison and Daniel near the entrance. Half the security guards were on the floor. A few were blocking the elevator, standing behind the investor, glaring at me with a mixture of exhaustion and satisfaction.

Something hit me in the face, and the next thing I knew I was on the ground. The guard that jumped over the table was on top of me, trying to hold me down. I thrust my elbow behind me, hitting his rib cage. It wasn't much, but it was enough to loosen his grip. I hooked his leg with mine attempting to get on top of him. Another guard came out of nowhere, kicking me in the side. I grunted.

The two guards grabbed my arms and hauled me to my feet, holding me tight against them. I knocked my head back and hit one in the jaw. With a small cry, a hand loosend from its grasp around my waist. I tried to turn to see my other opponent. A hand shot out and wrapped around my neck. I was stuck.

I looked over at Tanner, hoping to have some help. But none would come from him.

Even Tanner had a look of defeat. Tanner, who lets nothing get in his way. Allison and Daniel were new, but still. I glared at Mr. Bard, anger ready to explode as blood rushed to my cheeks and the veins in my neck pulsed. The guard had me in a choke hold. One wrong move and he could snap my neck. My face stung as blood seeped from my cut, the side of my head pounding. My mind flashed to the little girls that stared at me in terror, to Hailey, how she tried to protect me. I glanced at my team. I let them down.

I closed my eyes, letting out a sigh of defeat, knowing there was nothing I could do at that moment. Slowly, the man loosened his grip from my neck. He unzipped the bag and pulled out the Bayshire Stone. I narrowed my eyes at another guard that stood in front of me, clenching my fists until my knuckles turned white. Grabbing my arm in one hand and the stone in the other, he handed the stone to Mr. Bard, pulling me with him instead of letting go. "Is this what was stolen?" the guard asked.

"Yes," Randall Bard replied. "You know, I'm glad I forgot my keys."

"That thing is dangerous!" I shouted, trying to make him understand. I pulled at the guard's firm grip. He also had the brass knuckles laced through his fingers. My mind raced through the pages from the mission's file. Randall Bard never had a security detail. This shouldn't have happened. "You can't care for it properly here!"

"And you can?" he asked. "I funded the dig team, oversaw the entire procedure in discovering it, and have it *safely* in my care. How am I not being responsible, kid?" He practically hugged the Bayshire as he spoke. It sounded convincing, but I wasn't going to trust him because of a little speech.

"Are you aware of the dangers and problems that stone can create?" I asked.

"The Bayshire is not dangerous. It's a scientific breakthrough!" After he spoke, he looked at me inquisitively. "Who are you anyway?"

I looked over at Tanner, who grimaced in pain before shutting his eyes. "It doesn't matter who I am. I was sent to confiscate that artifact from you so no harm would come to anybody!" I tried to sound as authoritative as possible. Mr. Bard didn't even raise an eyebrow at what I said.

"You're not taking this from me. I don't care who sent you." The investor turned and stepped into the elevator. The doors shut behind him.

"No!" I shouted helplessly, still trapped within the guard's grasp, which felt like it was getting tighter by the second. I shook back and forth, failing to loosen his grip. A group of security guards blocked the elevator.

The guard tightened his grip on me even further, my hand going numb and my skin turning red. "Mr. Bard is an important man," the guard said. "If you follow him, you'll be dealing with a lot more than a couple scrapes and bruises." He shoved me away from him and stepped into the elevator. The worst part was that I believed him. No security guard would threaten to snap the neck of a minor.

"How could I let this happen?" I rubbed at my arm, which was red from the man's inhuman grip.

"It's not your fault, Alexis," Tanner said through clenched teeth.

I met his eyes. This was my fault. I looked at Tanner's leg, which was bent in an awkward position. He was hurt because of me. "That shouldn't have happened." I glared at the unopening doors of the elevator. "There is no reason we should have lost." I couldn't lose. I should have known it was too easy. "Let's just go back up there and force it from his hand."

Tanner looked at me. "Mills, it's not going to work." Was that pity in his eyes? No, it was understanding. He knew what I was thinking. At least he wasn't angry at me.

I sighed. I hated it when Tanner was right, which was usually always. I had an injured agent and two trainees who didn't know what to do. I was not emotionally prepared to go after the stone right now. I walked over to my team, grabbed Tanner's arm, and placed it over my shoulder. Daniel did the same, and we pulled him to his feet. Together we left the lobby, defeated.

Chapter 6
Gut Feeling

"You what?" Mr. Martial sat at his desk, his voice louder than his usual lectures. I didn't look at him. I couldn't.

"An agent was injured, and my team was unprepared to go after him again." I forced myself to meet his eyes.

"Agent Mills, this is unacceptable." Mr. Martial's voice was stern and cold. The lines across his forehead were glued in place. That was the problem with being a leader. You were the person who got blamed, especially when Mr. Martial was in charge.

"Yes, Sir." I stood up straight, my hands folded behind my back. "But, I think Mr. Bard knew we were coming." Mr. Martial was quiet. I had thought about it, and I couldn't let it go. I continued to speak. "There was an entire team of people waiting for us. They were trained in physical combat and dressed like security guards."

"How do you know they weren't actual security guards?" Mr. Martial asked.

I reran the fight in my head. "Security guards aren't trained to fight like they were. And they all wore these brass knuckles on their fingers," I said. "Not a security guard weapon. Not even a police officer's weapon. It's like they were waiting for us."

Mr. Martial sighed. "Do you have proof of that?"

"No. It's just a hunch," I said. "A gut feeling."

"A feeling?" Now I knew I messed up. "Agent Mills, we do not make assumptions based on a 'gut feeling.' We use our head and facts to make serious decisions like that." He punctuated every word.

"Sir, they were too well trained to just be security guards. They had no other reason to be there." Why wouldn't he listen to what I was saying? Mr. Martial wasn't going to agree with me. He never did.

"I think you have misunderstood the importance of this case, Agent Mills." Mr. Martial relaxed his tight grip on the rim of his desk.

"What do you mean?" I could feel my chest thumping.

"I'm taking you off the case."

"What!?" I shouted. My hands fell to my sides. How could he do this to me? I wanted to believe it wasn't my fault, but I wasn't sure if it was anymore. I should have been prepared for an ambush. I should have been ready. That was my job. But this wasn't fair. "Mr. Martial, I can get the stone back. It's not too late to go back for it!"

"I'm afraid it is. That was your one chance to prove you could be an instructor. The Bayshire is going on a tour through the country starting tomorrow."

"Then I'll go get it." Why hadn't I been told that before?

"I'm afraid it's not that simple. I will prepare a team of agents to retrieve the Bayshire. You're dismissed."

"But I want to be on that team."

Having an unfinished case put on my record was not acceptable. Dread clouded my senses. It was like the organization wouldn't see me as a top agent because Mr. Martial decided I wasn't good enough to complete this mission. I had to prove I was worthy of being an instructor.

"Agent Mills, keep training. I'll let you know when I have another assignment for you." Mr. Martial put his glasses on and focused his attention on his computer.

"What about camp?"

"I will take it up with the other directors. But you already know the requirements for the position."

"Sir, I want to be the Defense Tactics Instructor. It was just one case."

"Others might not agree. To be an instructor is to have new agents look up to you, to shape the next generation." As if I didn't know that already. "If you can't complete a simple assignment, then you won't make it as an instructor. I'm sorry."

"You're joking!" My whole body shook.

"Dismissed, Agent Mills."

Chapter 7
Agent Watson

I walked into the training room, threw my bag on the bench, and stormed around the room. I was still shaking from breaking and entering, from seeing those little girls, from Tanner getting hurt. How could Mr. Martial just take me off the case? I wanted to punch something.

"Must suck to be you." I spun around to the only person who could possibly make my day worse. "Mr. Perfect" was leaning against the wall, arms crossed, a sinister look plastered on his face. Damien Watson, the last person I wanted to see right now.

"You here to gloat or get your butt kicked?" I did my best to keep a straight face. If I lost my cool, Damien would never let it go. Why did he always show up at the worst times?

"I heard what happened. News travels fast." Damien ditched his place at the wall and strode over to me.

"I don't need your pity." I balled my fists.

"Clearly." Agent Watson snorted and took a step closer. "I'm just saying though, it can be hard when you're taken off a case."

"Just leave me alone, Damien."

"What are you going to do about it?" Damien stepped back, going into his fighting stance.

My mind went back to my time at the training camp when I first met Damien Watson. He was a jerk even back then.

It had been raining. There was a giant obstacle course. I was covered in mud from doing army crawls under barbed wire from the beginning of the course. My only actual competition was Damien.

We were near the end of the course. I pushed myself to go harder. All I had to do was run. I was almost there, almost at the finish line. I could smell the rain in the air. Out of nowhere, I went down, falling face-first into the mud. Damien laughed. He had tripped me to get in front. We could not touch another competitor.

It was challenging to pull myself out of the mud, but I managed. "Jerk!" I shouted back at him. I ran ahead with everything I had left and just barely made it through the finish line before him.

That started our feud for the rest of our training as he tried to beat me at everything. I didn't want his competition, but as the summer continued, it got worse and I couldn't ignore him or his taunts.

"Maybe I'll petition to be Defense Tactics Instructor," Watson said, pulling me back to the present, knowing that wasn't at all how it worked. He was still as a big a jerk as when we first met. And that statement proved it.

"We'll see about that." I grabbed my bag and left the training room, leaving Agent Watson by himself. The thought of him taking my position made me want to puke. I wanted more than anything to kick his butt, but I would just be giving him what he wanted. I would not lose control. I had to keep my emotions in check.

Chapter 8
Hailey

"Taken off the case, are you serious?" Miles asked. I slammed my locker shut. The last thing I needed right now was Miles getting angry on my behalf. There was enough anger going around already.

"I don't understand why either," I said. "It's not fair." I glared at the locker in front of me, wanting to punch its grey and gloomy surface. After failing my mission, I still had to go to school.

"Well, maybe Mr. Martial changed his mind. Maybe he has something else planned for you."

"It wasn't like that, Miles." I stopped talking for a moment as two kids walked past us. I couldn't wait for my junior year to be over, only a few days left. A few days to finish all of my finals while I sorted through what happened the day before. "He didn't listen to me," I continued, keeping my voice low. "I don't think the mission was as easy as he expected, and he didn't care about the information I had. But it's even more than that. He removed me from my position as instructor. At least, I think he's going to."

"Alexis, calm down." Miles smiled. I didn't realize how worked up I was. But I had a good reason to be. How could he be smiling right now? Someone walked up behind me. I turned to face a brown haired, brown-eyed girl who had the most welcoming smile on her face.

"What's up?" Sarah asked. Her innocent smile only made me more irritated. "Where were you this morning? You missed the first half of the day. And what happened to your face?"

Miles eyed me. "I slept in," I said, my hand reaching to the bandaid that covered the cut on my face. "I scratched it with my nails when I woke up," I lied.

Sarah shook her head at me. "You've got to stop doing that," she said looking at my nails. "At least you had the nerve to cut them afterwards." I rolled my eyes. I needed to come up with a new excuse.

"We're just talking about finals tomorrow," Miles said. I really wanted to tell Sarah about the T.S.O. I wanted my best friend to understand, but that wouldn't happen.

"Are you alright?" she asked.

"I'm fine. Come on, let's get to class." I eyed Miles before heading down the hall with Sarah.

"Okay, what's bothering you?" she asked. I shook my head. "Come on. You can't lie to me." If only she knew.

"I'm just thinking about Hailey," I said. Technically, I wasn't lying. That's the difficult thing about having a best friend who doesn't know you're a spy. You live undercover, trying to live between the lies. Sarah looked at me and put a hand on my shoulder. I tried to keep the memory away, but it came flooding back, making the back of my eyes burn.

I was only ten. Hailey, my older sister, was watching me while our parents were out. Three guys broke into the house. They threatened us. I could still hear Hailey's voice as the men dragged her out of the house, holding a gun to her. "Stay there, Alexis! Stay in the house!" she shouted.

I was crying, watching as the men who broke into my home threatened my sister's life. And for what? My mother's few pieces of nice jewelry and the couple hundred dollars saved for an emergency they had in the safe under their bed? Hailey tried to fight back, but she had no idea how to protect herself. She died trying to save me while I stood there and watched. I should have done something.

After they killed Hailey, I started learning how to fight, and fight well. When I was recruited by the T.S.O. I devoted every day of my life to avenging her death in the only way I knew how. I put everything I had into stopping people like the men who killed her. It's why I wanted to be an instructor. People needed to know how to protect themselves, and I wanted to teach them.

"It's not your fault," Sarah said. I didn't answer. "Hey." I looked at her and stopped walking. My muscles relaxed a little. "Everything's going to be okay," she said. I smiled. Even when Sarah didn't have a clue about what was going on, she always seemed to know what to say.

We walked into the classroom, and I slid into my seat. I couldn't just give up on the case. I had to do something. I didn't give up on my sister. I learned to protect myself and promised to fight to protect others. I couldn't give up on this case either. There was no way I could let it go, not that easily. And it wasn't about being the Defense Tactics Instructor, not all of it. That case was still mine. I had a job to finish.

Chapter 9
Decisions

"Well?" Tanner asked. "What are you going to do?" I stood between Tanner and Miles in front of the school. Everyone wanted to know what I was going to do, but I didn't know if my answer was the right one. Tanner was leaning on a crutch, a boot on his left foot. It was my reminder I messed up, and that he paid for it. I couldn't look at it. As much as I wanted to look at Tanner and have him smile back at me with his blue eyes, I couldn't make eye contact. It was my fault he was hurt.

"I don't know," I said. "But I'm not done yet."

"Alexis." I looked up at Miles. "Ignore what Mr. Martial said."

I stared at Miles as I failed to comprehend what he said. "Did Miles just ask me to ignore my director?" I asked. Tanner even looked shocked at Miles' remark. He never disobeyed anything. Ever.

"Come on, Alexis. You already know what you have to do," Miles said. His enthusiasm lifted my spirits. Tanner sat down at the bench behind him. He looked at me. We had one of those silent understandings. We were both still surprised with Miles's comment, but Tanner knew what was right. I couldn't give up.

Sarah walked up behind us. "Do what they say, Alexis," she said to me.

"You don't even know what's going on," I said, looking back and forth between all of them. I smiled, my heart racing at the idea of disobeying Mr. Martial. That's why Sarah was my best friend. She was completely clueless about what was going on around her, but she supported me anyway, without question.

"I don't need to," she said. "If it's big enough for Miles to tell you to break the rules, then it has to be important." Sarah shrugged her shoulders.

Miles raised his eyebrows at me. I knew they were right, but I was told to leave it alone. I didn't know what to do. If I was caught disobeying orders, it could be the end for me.

"Well, I've got to get home, but you'll figure it out," Sarah reassured me. "Whatever it is." She walked away.

"Alexis?" Tanner asked.

I shifted my weight and sighed. Yesterday was the first time I had been caught on a job. It wasn't a good feeling. "I don't want to get fired," I said. "Besides, the Bayshire is on tour." Way to go, Alexis. Now you're coming up with excuses.

"I'm pretty sure you can find out where it's going," Miles said.

I looked at Tanner for support. "You're too good of an agent for them to fire you that easily."

I silently thanked him for his encouragement. What would I do without him? If I went after the stone and failed, I would be in trouble for sure. But if I succeeded... Mr. Martial couldn't get rid of me for finishing a mission on my own directive, could he? They might even give me back my position as instructor.

If I did this wrong, I could lose everything. But if I did it right… At least I'd have a chance.

It was a chance I was willing to take.

Opening my laptop, I searched for the Bayshire's tour schedule. The Smithsonian Museum of Natural History was the first on the list, but the stone was only going to be there until the end of next week, which was the end of finals for me.

"Find anything?" Miles asked, poking his head inside the office cube. If only I had my own office, like the agents at headquarters.

"I think so," I said. Miles looked over my shoulder at the computer. "It's leaving the Smithsonian at the end of the week, but its next location is in Texas."

"Then I guess you know where you need to go."

"But how am I going to get there? I'm not supposed to go after it. The T.S.O. isn't going to pay for a flight or give my parents a reason why I'm gone. I can't expect the T.S.O. to be of any help. And my mom will be difficult to get on board, especially with school just ending."

"What if you got an exclusive invite to go on an out-of-state field trip with your school, fully funded?" Miles asked. "As an end of the year trip. I can work something out."

"That's not a bad idea." I smiled and let the idea sink in. "Still though, how am I going to get to Texas?"

"Alexis, you're a secret agent. Are you telling me you're going to let transportation get in your way?"

"Well, when you put it like that," I said. Miles was right. I was overthinking unimportant details. Getting a plane ticket was probably the easiest part of this whole thing.

"There's the Alex I know." Miles patted me on the back. I rolled my eyes at his nickname, but he ignored it.

"Now I need to convince my parents."

Chapter 10
Once in A Lifetime

"Mom, why can't I go?" I asked, following her around the kitchen counter. I was getting a headache from all of her pacing.

"Alexis, I'm sorry. I don't have enough time for you to go on a three-day trip to Texas next week!" Mom exclaimed. When she put it like that, I could see how silly it sounded. "I don't have a way to pay for it. How come I haven't heard about this sooner?" She put her glass down on the counter and turned to face me, her hand on her hip.

"Mom, this is a once in a lifetime opportunity, and it's already paid for." I threw my hands out to my sides. I didn't mean to raise my voice, but I really needed her to agree to this. Dad was the easy parent.

"A prepaid trip? Now why doesn't that sound convincing?" Mom asked me sarcastically.

"I'm not lying." I handed her the papers that had all the information and the plane ticket. Miles helped me forge documents back at the office. I silently thanked him for his ingenious idea. But it was all going to be for nothing if Mom didn't say yes.

"What exactly is this trip for?" She looked the papers over, finally thinking about the possibility. "And what about your finals?"

"We will visit museums and historical sites in Houston. It will be really educational, like an end of the year field trip. Besides, school is over next week. Finals will be over. The trip is next weekend when school is over. Please, Mom," I pleaded. I stuck out my bottom lip and folded my hands. I had to sell this to her, to the last cell in my body.

Mom sighed. "I'll have to talk to your dad." Yes! That meant she was really considering it, and Dad rarely said no to these once in a lifetime opportunities.

"Thanks, Mom." I gave her a hug before running back to my room.

That night, I listened to my parents discuss the trip in their room. I stood outside the closed door, listening carefully, silently. Dad got home from work late. He was tired. This could work in my favor.

"I say let her go," Dad said in his tired voice.

"Are you sure?" Mom asked. *Yes, he's sure!* I wanted to say.

"It's totally paid for with school funds, and Alexis has never been to Texas. I think it would be fun for her."

There was a moment of silence. From my spot outside their door, I held my breath, the steady beating of my heart burning in my ears.

"Alright then," Mom said. "I guess she would enjoy it. And she deserves a little vacation." I let myself breathe. If only it were a vacation.

Finals were over, so now I could focus entirely on getting the Bayshire Stone. Mom and Dad dropped me off at school. This was going to be great. All I had to do was get to

Texas, grab the stone from the museum, and walk it into Mr. Martial's office. Piece of cake. Right?

"Where is everyone else?" Dad asked. He and Mom climbed out of the car and stood beside me.

"Probably not here yet," I said, holding back my excitement. Where was he? A car pulled in and stopped behind them. Miles got out, grabbed a backpack, and came to stand beside me.

"Oh. Miles is going too!" Mom smiled. "Perfect!"

Miles waved at her. "Hi Mrs. Mills."

A school bus entered the parking lot and pulled up to the curb a few feet away from our cars. "That's us," I said. We planned this perfectly.

The school's football coach stepped off the bus. There was an after school celebration off campus for the football team, and they got their coach to get a bus for them to travel together. It was perfect, because Mom and Dad didn't know anything about it.

"Well, have a good time guys," Dad said. The coach caught sight of us and waved. Dad waved back, smiling. They pulled me into a tight hug and got back into their car.

"Bye!" I shouted, waving to my parents as they drove out of the school parking lot.

I turned to Miles. "You ready?" he asked. I wished it was Tanner driving, but it didn't matter. Besides, Miles wasn't coming with me like my parents thought. That would be too risky. He was just my ride.

I opened the car door and stepped inside, dropping my duffel bag at my feet. Miles got in the driver's seat and threw his empty backpack in the back seat. Of course I was ready. I tapped my foot against my bag, unable to keep still. "Let's get out of here," I said, adorning a pair of sunglasses.

"You got it." Miles started the car, and we made our way to the airport.

Step one completed. I had a trip planned that went completely against my orders. I was going to be in a ton of trouble when I got back.

"Alright," Miles started. "Let's go over everything." He drove into the airport and stopped at the passenger drop-off.

"I'm there on a field trip. If a T.S.O. agent sees me or recognizes me, I'm simply there visiting their base. Miles, I'll be fine."

"I'm just covering all the bases before you leave."

"Miles, I basically live undercover. I think I can handle myself." I rolled my eyes, but he couldn't tell through the sunglasses.

I stepped out of the car then pulled my bag out. "See you, Alex!" Miles called after me.

"Don't call me that!" I peeked inside the open window. Miles shook his head at me. "See you in a few days." I stepped away from the curb, and he drove off.

Entering the airport, I went through security and took my seat on the plane. Once we were in the air, I put on my headphones and leaned back against the chair, letting everything else fade away into the clouds.

Off to find the Bayshire Stone.

Chapter 11
Coffee, Bagels, and Spies

"Attention passengers, we have reached our destination." I took my headphones off and stuffed them in my bag. "The current time here in Houston is ten sixteen," the voice over the intercom said. I grabbed the blueprint of the museum from my lap and stuffed it in my bag.

We were still in the air. I could see the land below us as it crept closer. The tall buildings of Houston, Texas colored the ground below me. My heart raced. My ears popped.

"Here we go."

Once the plane landed, I gathered my things and left the aircraft. How much trouble would I be in if I was caught? What if things went wrong? Would my career be over? What would I do then? No. I couldn't think like that. I had to stay focused. I had to accomplish this mission. Alexis doesn't quit. There was no turning back now. I thought about Miles and how much he helped me get here, even though it could jeopardize his place at the T.S.O. I couldn't let all this be for nothing. I thought about Tanner. He was probably taking charge of distracting my parents for the duration of the trip. It had been a long time since I worked a mission without a partner. The Bayshire Stone would be off exhibit tonight and ready to head to its next location tomorrow morning. This was the closest flight I could manage without raising too many questions from the T.S.O. or my parents. I sent them a text to let them know I arrived safely.

I only had today.

I left the airport and took a bus into town. With my bag in my lap, I stared at buildings flying past the dirty window.

"Have you been to Houston before?"

I turned away from the window and faced the person seated next to me. A woman probably in her late forties was staring at me. She had a round face, blond hair, and round glasses covering her hazel eyes.

"No, it's my first time." Was it usual for strangers to talk on the bus? If only I had my driver's license. I couldn't wait for Driver's Ed! "It's really big though," I said. I stared out the window at the towering buildings looming over us. Avoiding questions from adults usually led to more trouble.

"Are you by yourself?" she asked.

"I have family here that I'm visiting for awhile." I wondered if Miles would glare at me right now for changing my story. But being alone on a city bus doesn't exactly scream school field trip.

I looked away from her, not sure if I should continue the conversation. Thankfully, the woman didn't ask any more questions. I thought for a moment about what I said, visiting family. It had become so easy to lie, to make up stories on the spot. I had become reliant on it.

The first lie I told was about the training camp. I had to tell my parents something believable. Because I had been learning physical combat since Hailey died, I told my parents

I was going to a Krav Maga camp. It worked, and that's all that mattered.

The bus pulled to a stop. I grabbed my things and headed down the street. A coffee shop stood at the end of the corner. Perfect.

The café wasn't crowded, much to my advantage. The abstract paintings on the walls were paired with closeups of coffee cups. Light jazz music was playing, but I was too preoccupied to focus on it. The room smelled of fresh coffee and something sweet. It reminded me of the coffee shop back in Ohio. I ordered a coffee and bagel and found an empty seat at the back of the shop. I called Miles.

"Did you make it?" he asked over the phone.

"Houston is huge. How's everything over there?" I took a bite of my bagel.

"Alexis, it's only been a few hours since you left."

"True." I took a sip of my coffee and pulled it back, burning my tongue.

"Okay, let's go over the plan."

I rolled my eyes. He worried too much.

"I just want to make sure you're ready," he said. Like he knew I was mocking him for being too precautious. He knew me too well. I was ready to do this, to take the Bayshire to the Ohio base and show Mr. Martial I'm capable of doing anything he might throw at me.

"I enter the museum," I started. "It'll probably be crowded so I won't seem suspicious. The Bayshire is on exhibit in the Gottesman Hall of Earth. It will be in a glass case with built-in motion detectors and heat sensors. But there is a silent alarm for it hooked up to a different system." I really wished Tanner was there to help me with the technical stuff. I pictured him and his injured leg. It was good he wasn't here. I couldn't see him get hurt anymore.

"More coffee?" the waitress asked.

44

"No thanks," I said, looking up from my phone. The waitress eyed me as she walked away. Was everyone out to get me?

"What?" Miles asked as the waitress left.

"Sorry, nothing." I pulled out my notebook and looked at the floor plans of the museum.

"How are you going to get it out?" Miles asked.

His interest in my mission felt a little odd, but I appreciated the support. It was Tanner I usually have these conversations with. For a moment I wondered why it wasn't him on the phone, but I let the thought pass. At least I wasn't completely on my own.

"I have two options." I scrunched my nose, thinking about how to get the stone out of the glass case. I was never one to prepare everything ahead of time. These were options I came up with on the plane. "Option one: I hack into the security system and deactivate the silent alarm. Once I'm alone in the room, I use my acid pen to create a hole in the glass and get the stone." I thought about the pen for a moment. It was an exceptional tool. "The downfall is the heat from the pen might disrupt the heat sensors inside the case, which are controlled manually from a box under the stone's case. I would have to deactivate that first, but I probably wouldn't have much time alone before I get caught."

"And option two?"

"Option two is…I set off the fire alarm." I adjusted the plan as I said it, imagining what could happen in my head. I did this often, and it drove people nuts. Yeah, it's why I got in trouble in the first place, but what good was being a secret agent if you couldn't improvise? I'm pretty sure what happened at the penthouse proved you couldn't prepare for every situation. "The place will be evacuated," I said. "From under the glass case, I can deactivate the heat sensor system. With enough time, I can pry the case open, which leaves less evidence."

"Alexis, you know those are basically the same plan, right?"

"Miles, please."

"And the problem with the second plan?" Miles asked.

"I don't want to get involved with any law enforcement, or be caught by a T.S.O. agent. Mr. Martial said a team would be sent for the stone." There wasn't any news at base about the Bayshire, so I knew they hadn't retrieved it yet. But working against my own people would not be easy. "It could take too much time. Time I won't have."

"I suggest you set off the fire alarm to clear the room, deactivate both security systems, then pry open the case," Miles said. "By the way, I left you something in your duffel bag that should help."

I opened my bag and rifled through my things. There was a small device, almost like a CD.

"It's from Tanner. One of his 3D hologram projectors. It might help you buy some time. It's already been coded with an image of the Bayshire."

"Awesome," I said, putting the device back. I thought about Tanner, then his messed-up foot. If I hadn't been blinded by the simplicity of retrieving the stone the first time, he wouldn't have gotten hurt. And I wouldn't have to be in Texas right now. I guess it really was my fault.

How did Miles even get the device in my bag in the first place? I didn't bother asking. He was a spy, after all.

I hung up the phone and finished my bagel. It was twelve-thirty. A fifteen-minute bus ride would take me to the museum. My coffee mug was empty. My stomach was churning with excitement.

My heart stopped. I watched the waitress from the corner of my eye. She pulled a metal ring out from her apron. No, not a ring. One of those brass knuckles. I was being watched. I grabbed my bag and ran to the bathroom before she turned around. And Mr. Martial said my gut wasn't trustworthy.

In front of the mirror, I pulled a blonde wig out of my duffel bag, tucking my brown hair inside it. I pulled out a makeup pallet and did what I could to change my features. I pushed a button on my bag hidden in the zipper. The black duffel bag changed to a dark purple. If Mr. Bard was here, I did not want him recognizing me. And I definitely didn't want the waitress following me. No matter how bad getting caught by another agent would be, being stopped by Mr. Bard was one hundred times worse. I had been in Texas not even an hour, and already I had people on my tail. That had to be a new record or something.

Chapter 12
Gottesman Hall of Earth

I slipped my acid pen into my pocket and attached my pocket knife to a hidden slot in my belt. The decoder was in my duffel bag, along with the gloves Mr. Martial had given me for handling the stone, and Tanner's holographic device. I had enough money to buy a ticket to the museum in my pocket, along with my phone and badge.

I slipped past the waitress and out of the coffee shop while she fussed over a table on the opposite wall. From my place at the bus stop, I watched her rush out of the shop, look up and down the street, then storm back in. Was the woman from the bus also working for Mr. Bard? On the bus, I stared out the window while my imagination overloaded itself with ideas. Mr. Bard had to be close by. This time, I had to be ready.

It was a big museum. A huge green lawn covered the front of the property. Entering the building, I bought my ticket and headed to the Gottesman Hall of Earth exhibit at the back of the museum. My face felt hot, and my hands were shaking, waiting for action.

There weren't many people in the exhibit. With my bag slung over my shoulder, I headed down the hall into the large room. The moment I stepped inside, a large banner hanging from the ceiling caught my attention. A photo of the Bayshire Stone, in all it's glory, was plastered against a navy-blue background.

I wondered why the stone would be on exhibit if it was so dangerous. It didn't seem safe to haul it across the country just to make some money. Mr. Bard had some sort of plan, deeper than his pockets. I just had to figure out what it was, after I fixed this mess.

I walked under the banner into the middle of the room. The entire corner on the far side of the room was designated to the Bayshire Stone. I erased all the other artifacts from my vision. There was a video playing on the wall behind me, but I couldn't hear what was being said.

The only thing that mattered to me right now was getting the Bayshire. Then I could worry about my position. I imagined the look on Mr. Martial's face when I brought the stone into headquarters. Agent Watson would probably sneer for whatever twisted reason he had. But the most important thing? I would be recognized as an agent that got the job done and was reliable.

I walked towards the exhibit.

Plaques on the wall described the scientific importance of the stone and how it was capable of high levels of electricity. Another section had an image of an explosion. Interesting. I read the story.

When the Bayshire was first retrieved from the excavation site, it was brought into the nearest town for study. A team of scientists worked to uncover as much information as possible. They put the unknown object through various tests to decipher what it was made of. When the team of scientists attempted to extract a small sample,

49

the Bayshire glowed. Within a minute, all the electrical equipment in the lab began to vibrate. The entire building and half the block lost power. Before the scientists could detect the cause, an MRI machine in the room next-door exploded.

An intern working in the room died from the explosion. A few others, including the research team working with the Bayshire, were badly injured.

We still don't know how the Bayshire could cause such a significant electrical charge to cause the MRI machine to explode. Since then, no one has been allowed to do any further testing.

I looked back at the rock inside the case I was about to open and marveled at the destruction this little thing could cause. It definitely shouldn't be on display out in public after causing such damage. Next to the story was a poster of the investor and a short bio explaining his life's work and ownership of the Bayshire Stone. It wasn't impressive. How did Randall Bard ever get permission to have the stone in his personal care? It belonged in some place where people who hungered for power couldn't touch it. If this little rock was capable of that much damage, I understood why it had to be protected by the T.S.O.

I browsed through everything else in the exhibit, trying to make myself look busy. I needed the right moment. Along with the stone was a case that held some dig tools used at the excavation site. Two people walked up to the Bayshire and began reading. A few other people were busy in other parts of the room.

I couldn't activate the fire alarm without being noticed. And first responders would most-likely go straight to the room the alarm came from. Looking over my shoulder at the stone, I left the room and stepped into the exhibit further down the hall. It was a large room, and there weren't any people close enough to notice me.

I found the fire alarm. It was mounted on the wall beside the emergency exit. I strolled over to it, my heart jumping inside my body with nerves, ready for action. I took a deep breath, reached out my hand, and pulled down on the bar.

Chapter 13
Fire

The loud blaring alarm filled the museum. The ringing made my ears buzz. "What's going on?" a woman shouted from across the room.

"Fire!" I shouted, my voice on the verge of breaking.

Someone in the room screamed as they all ran for the emergency exit. I pretended to follow them out the door. Once the exit was shut, I ran from the room, dashed back through the hallway, back into the other exhibit, and skidded to a stop in front of the Bayshire Stone.

"Time to get to work."

I laid my duffel bag on the floor beside the Bayshire. With the fire alarm going off, I didn't worry about making too much noise. The alarm blended into the background inside my head. I pulled out my laptop and plugged in a flash drive. Opening up the T.S.O. system, I easily hacked into the museum's security system. I hoped Miles was covering my tracks back at the base, erasing my log-on info.

With the cameras shut down and the motion-activated alarms dead, I grabbed my decoding device and slid my head under the glass case to see. The bottom half of the case was covered in a red cloth. Under the case, I plugged my device into the control switch and shut it down.

I put the device back in my bag and pulled out a small metal stick, the T.S.O.'s version of a crowbar, only much cooler. The case was designed especially for the Bayshire, to prevent it from causing any damage or being exposed to anything. The top piece of glass was fitted perfectly to the sides. There was a keyhole to open a door just big enough to get the stone out from one of the side panels. I thought about using my key card to open the hatch instead. No, I might need it later.

The alarm stopped blaring. I was running out of time. I pried the metal stick between the glass and slowly lifted the top piece.

I didn't realize I was holding my breath.

"Got it," I whispered. There was no time to worry about wearing protective gloves. I lifted the stone out of the case, careful not to hit the sides. The stone felt cold and heavy. I held it for a moment, worried my touch might cause something to happen. But nothing did.

"Hey!"

I spun around. A security guard stood in the doorway. The museum's logo was stitched onto his uniform. Mr. Bard stood next to him. Wonderful.

I stuffed the stone in my bag and slung it around my shoulder. No point for a fake hologram.

I thought about saluting the two men, saying something snarky before dashing out the door. Probably best I didn't.

Thrusting the emergency doors open, I dashed across the large field. Darting through the few trees near the walkway, I headed across the grass towards the parking lot.

"Stop!" The guard shouted.

What if I showed him my badge? Would that do anything against the word of Mr. Bard? But then I looked at his face. It was the same man that attacked me, that had me in a choke hold in the penthouse, only in a different uniform. Definitely not a security guard then. Now I knew. They were Randall Bard's personal guards. I kept running.

I risked a look behind me as I ran. The man was close, Mr. Bard not far behind him.

Something rammed into my shoulder.

Two people dressed like more security guards wrestled me to the ground. My duffel bag went flying as I hit the grass. They held my arms down, but my right leg was free. I kicked upwards, hitting one of them in the chest. He let go of my arm and rolled over with a grunt. I whipped my arm around and punched the other man in the chin. It knocked his head back, but he didn't lose his grip. All of my training flooded through my mind.

Putting all the force in my legs, I wrapped myself around him. He let go of my arm and balled his left hand into a fist. Before he could hit me, I jabbed my elbow into his collar bone, my legs pushing his weight off me.

I jumped up and looked across the grass for my bag. Someone grabbed me from behind and held me. I thrust my foot down and elbowed whoever was holding me, but they didn't budge. Instead, the person grabbed my elbows and pulled them farther behind my back, twisting my arm. It was the man with the inhuman grip. I grimaced.

Randall Bard stepped towards my bag, which was lying in the grass a few feet in front of me. He pulled the Bayshire out of my bag and smiled at me.

"You don't understand," I said, trying to wriggle out of the man's grasp.

"I suggest you leave now, Agent Mills. Before you get arrested." Agent Mills? Mr. Bard knew who I was? Even with the disguise, of course, it wasn't a very good one. How did he know my name? I never told him. How did he know I was going to be here? He saw the confused expression on my face and laughed. "Ah, you see. There are things I know that you don't. Dangerous things. Now. I suggest you leave. Before things get messy. This is your last chance."

"I can't leave without the Bayshire." I pretended to struggle in the man's grasp. Mr. Bard threw the duffel bag at my feet.

"Yes, you can. And you will." Mr. Bard turned away from me, stone in hand. "Good day, Agent Mills," he sang and headed back towards the museum.

I moved. It was like a movie, and I got lost in the fight's rhythm. First, I knocked my head back, then took the man's loosened grasp to my advantage, elbowing him in the rib cage. He crumpled on the grass, holding his broken nose.

I ran for Mr. Bard. His guards blocked me from running any further. Someone hit me in the shoulder, then two of them grabbed at me and held me in place. I watched Mr. Bard, wishing I could hit his perfectly tanned nose, as he walked back inside the museum. I struggled to loosen the men's hold on me, but I was outnumbered. As soon as the investor was back inside the building, they shoved me towards the ground. I lost the stone. Again.

There was no way I could walk back into that museum.

I stumbled, but I didn't fall. I charged towards them again, unwilling to give up. With my heavy field boots, I thrust my foot down on one man. I raised my leg to kick another, to keep fighting, but the man I was aiming at thrust his own boot into my gut before I could see it. I fell to the ground, the wind knocked out of me. I looked past them. Back at the emergency exit, more guards walked out. I wouldn't be able to get past them, not without backup, not without getting seriously hurt. "I told you to stay out of it," the guard from the penthouse growled at me. "Leave now, or you'll be leaving in pieces."

I pulled myself to my feet. "I know you think I'm the bad guy, but I'm not." I spit the words out at them. They left a sour taste in my mouth. They stared at me, blinking without a single emotion.

I tugged on my gloves, grabbed my bag, and backed away. I needed a new angle, one where I wouldn't end up dead before getting home. I passed by two firetrucks, watching as confused men and women in firefighter uniforms walked out of the building.

I messed up. Again.

Chapter 14
Lectures from Friends

I sat at a bus station, cell phone in hand. I discarded the blonde wig in a trash can a few blocks away. My duffel bag was back to its normal black.

"Did you get it?" Miles asked. Even over the phone, I could hear the hopefulness in his voice. I sighed and looked down the street in front of me. "What happened?" he asked.

"Mr. Bard showed up. I would have had it if he and his goons didn't mess with me!"

"Alexis, stop shouting."

I took a deep breath, balling and unballing my fists. Staying calm wasn't happening right now. If I didn't figure out how to fix this, I definitely wasn't going to be a Defense Tactics Instructor. This whole thing was a waste. "What am I supposed to do now?" I asked.

"The stone's next location is in California. At the Glayfield Museum."

"Isn't that where Headquarters is?" I asked. I let myself hope that was a good thing. I really needed a positive.

If there was a way to come out of this unscathed, I was going to take it.

"Yes. Headquarters is in California," Miles clarified. I nodded my head, knowing I didn't have a lot of choices left. It was either go to California and try again or go home, accept defeat, and lose the stone. That wasn't an option.

"Fine. Okay." A bus pulled up to the stop. Two people got off. I stayed put on the bench. "Miles, can you arrange a flight for me to Glayfield, California?"

"Looking at flights right now. There's one in about two hours. You'll have a seat by the time you get to the airport."

I hung up the phone.

California.

I hadn't been there since Training Camp. I thought back to the first day I learned about the T.S.O. My time at the Training Camp flashed through my mind. I remembered the rock wall during Physical Training, where I fell and messed up my left leg. I had a very big, very unpretty scar across the back of my calf. At the end of the day, I was proud of my injury. It proved I would go as far as necessary to get the job done.

Just like I was now. As far as California.

Then there were my old friends. Amelia Zegro, or Agent Z. Emily, or Agent Steinfeld. We worked together during our drills and became a powerful team when we were at camp. They were stationed in California at T.S.O. Headquarters. I hadn't thought about them for a very long time.

Once the next bus arrived, I rode back to the airport.

Chapter 15
Welcome to California

The stone still had almost a week before arriving in California. What was I supposed to do in that extra time?

I turned the volume up on my headphones. If only I could forget about everything. I wasn't expecting this case to bring back terrible memories. I had been on the plane for an hour. Two more hours to go before landing. The T.S.O. Subway Station had a stop at the airport that would take me to Headquarters in Glayfield. I thought of Ms. Blanchard, the T.S.O. Headquarters Director. Did she know about me being taken off the case? Of course she did. She was the Director. She knew about everything that happened in the T.S.O. It was her job to know.

I looked out the window at the afternoon sky. The clouds below the wing of the airplane were mesmerizing. It was like an ocean of white, protecting me from all the danger back on the ground. It was peaceful up here. There was no T.S.O., no Bayshire Stone, no position at the training camp on the line, no thoughts about my sister's death. Just me and my music. I leaned my head back on the seat and listened to the fast-paced words of the song.

When the plane landed, I grabbed my bag and headed towards the security area on the second floor.

I stopped near a small food market, people swarming around me. A man in a black sweatshirt, hood covering his face, stopped across the aisle and picked up a book from a shelf. Something felt odd about him. A tug deep in my gut told me to be wary. He looked familiar, but I couldn't tell why. Something about his posture, maybe. Maybe he was on my plane? I pushed the thought aside and took the escalator to the second floor.

I kept walking, but an uneasy feeling made the hairs on the back of my neck stand up. I glanced behind me and tensed. There he was again, about two yards behind me. The man in the hoodie.

I was being followed.

Instead of going to the Security Station, where I could take an elevator to the T.S.O. Subway, I stopped in the women's bathroom. In the mirror, I looked more tired than I thought. Exhaustion crept in from all the excitements and disappointments. I had been going non-stop since I woke up this morning back in Ohio. And being on two different airplanes didn't help. Splashing some water on my face, I perked myself up.

"Just get the stone. Then head back to Ohio. Nothing to it," I said under my breath, hyping myself up.

If only Miles or Tanner were here to watch my back. Never mind them. I'm strong enough to do this on my own. More than strong enough. I would not fail again. I couldn't. I looked at myself in the mirror and tightened my ponytail. I didn't need any help. I didn't need to put anyone else in danger. I was going to get out of this airport without being seen, get the stone, then become the Defense Tactics Instructor after getting it back to the base. Nothing to it.

I peeked my head out the bathroom door. No one was there. I stepped out, further down the way where the market place was, the same guy was standing by the closest shop. Was he another one of Mr. Bard's minions? If only I could see his face. He carried a small backpack slung over his shoulder. He squatted and started pulling books from a small shelf outside the store. Now was my chance.

I dashed in the opposite direction towards the exit.

Approaching the security station, I slid to a stop. The black hoodie was nowhere in sight. I lost him.

"Sorry, Miss." A security guard blocked my path, right hand raised to stop me. "You can't go back this way." I looked the man up and down, still catching my breath. There was always a guard at almost every airport in the country who was an undercover agent. They wore a special pin on their uniform so other agents would recognize them. This man was who I was looking for.

On his left shoulder, under the sewn-on security badge, was a small pin. It was the T.S.O. logo, just small enough for agents to recognize it, but discrete enough so the normal citizen would never notice it.

I pulled out my badge. "Agent Mills," I said, looking him in the eye.

The security guard gave me a slight nod. "Door's that way," he said, eyes unwavering. He pointed to a door on my left, hidden from view by a metal detector. I nodded and walked to the door. No one else paid any attention to me. The door had a security personnel sign posted on it. Turning the knob, I entered a breakroom, decked out with a table, a mini kitchen, and a TV on the wall. There was another door on the wall to my right. Perfect.

I slid through the other door, entering a small space. Flipping the light switch only provided minimal visibility. Cleaning equipment that threatened to topple over any second filled shelves along the back wall. I stepped up to the empty space beside the shelves and placed my hand on the icy surface. A green light appeared beside my hand. A section of the wall slid away from view, and I stepped into the space.

The elevator took me four stories below ground level. With a quiet ding, the door opened, and I stepped onto the subway platform. A silver tinted three-car subway train waited for me on the tracks. I took a seat close to the doors and resisted the urge to close my eyes. A man sat across from me, eyeing me carefully.

"What?" I barked, always on my toes. He wasn't working for Mr. Bard too, was he? He shook his head, clinging tightly to the computer on his lap, moving his thumbs. "Nervous about something?" I asked.

"Not at all." He smiled at me, his eyes looking deep into mine. He creeped me out. He didn't look like an agent, considering how he fidgeted in his seat and watched me like I was the enemy. But if he was on this train, he worked for the T.S.O. I had nothing to worry about. I turned to the empty window and waited for the train to arrive at Headquarters.

Chapter 16
Mr. O'Neil

My stomach was turning by the time the subway came to a stop. I hadn't eaten anything since the café in Texas. There were sleeping quarters provided at Headquarters for agents at any time. I could stay there, get some rest and shower. Then I could focus on getting the Bayshire Stone.

Once the doors opened, I headed towards the visitor center. I had to sign in if I wanted to bunk here, which meant my location would go on record. But I didn't have much choice. I needed a place to stay. With my bag slung over my shoulder, I stood tall and walked with purpose.

The other man on the train ended up at the same destination as me. He walked with his head low, computer tucked under his arm. He approached the desk at the check-in center. I waited, watching him. Something was off about him, but I couldn't place it.

"Where am I supposed to go?" the man asked.

"Name?" The woman at the desk looked up at him.

"Mr. O'Neil. I'm a new computer technician."

"I see." The woman at the desk typed something into her computer. "Here you are. You're stationed in section F. Just take the hall on your left and you'll find it. Welcome to the T.S.O." she said.

"Thank you."

The man walked away, and I stepped up to the desk. After signing in, I made my way towards the bunking area. It was a one-person room. My name was already posted on the digital sign on the door. Agent Mills. I placed my hand on the visible scanner and entered my bunk.

There was a twin-sized bed, a desk, a small dresser, and a small closet. Next to the closet was the door to a small bathroom. The walls were painted a simple grey, much like the rest of the place. The T.S.O. didn't care very much for décor, did they?

With a heavy sigh, I threw my bag on the bed and called Miles. My foot tapped against the hard floor as I waited for him to answer.

"You need to be careful, Alexis."

"I'm aware Miles, thank you." There was silence on the other line. "Do you have anything for me?"

"The Bayshire will be there in three days from today, at the Glayfield Earth and Space Museum. It will be on exhibit all of next week."

In Texas, going after the stone in broad daylight didn't work. A plan formed in my head. "Maybe this time I should try to get it before it goes on exhibit," I said.

"That might work."

I wouldn't have to worry about a huge diversion like I did in Texas. No one else would be around, and I wouldn't be in plain sight. But I would have some other problems with having to break into the museum's storage facility. It would be worth the risk.

I hung up with Miles and wandered the halls until I found the gym. Maybe I could get a workout in, take my frustration out on a punching bag. A group of newer agents was being drilled on self-defense techniques. I imagined myself as the instructor, my agents-in-training watching me intently, studying my every move, and committing it to memory. Was the position at camp something I had in my future anymore? I was afraid to know the answer. The thought made me queesy.

I didn't want to interrupt the class or draw attention to myself, so I headed back to my room and took a hot shower. After I was freshened up, I walked to the cafeteria and grabbed some dinner before I let myself crash on the squeaky bed.

Chapter 17
Director Blanchard

I woke up to a voice coming from the intercom in my room. "Agent Mills, you are needed in the Director's office."

Me? In Ms. Blanchard's office? That's not good. She had to know I wasn't supposed to be here. The last time I saw her was at graduation from the T.S.O. Training Camp. Was she going to send me back to Ohio empty-handed? Inform Mr. Martial I was here? I couldn't let that happen.

Mr. Martial may be strict, but everyone knew about Ms. Blanchard, California's Base Director, the Director of the T.S.O. Headquarters. She ran a tight ship and expected everyone to take their job as seriously as she did. She was not a force you wanted to reckon with.

What did Ms. Blanchard want?

I sprang from the bed and quickly changed my clothes. I slipped my arms through my leather jacket, pulled on my fingerless gloves, and tied back my hair as I rushed out the door and hurried down the hallway.

My feet froze in front of Ms. Blanchard's door, my hand levitating above the doorknob. I was about to see the

Director. The head of T.S.O. Headquarters. My blood felt like ice in my veins as my breath seemed to freeze in my throat. Keep it together. Everything was going to be fine. I hoped.

I stood up taller and pulled my gloves down further on my hands, letting the tension from the leather in between my fingers pull me back to reality.

Ms. Blanchard's office was spotless. Unlike my room at home, everything was organized and had its proper place. It even smelled nice, like a pine tree.

"Agent Mills," Ms. Blanchard said, looking up at me from a file on her desk. I folded my hands behind my back and stared at her, expressionless.

"Good morning, Director," I said.

"I hope your secret trip went well." She knew why I was here. That had to mean Mr. Martial knew too, right? My heartbeat sped up, and I struggled to keep my heart from leaping out of my chest.

"Director, if I may-"

"You may not." Ms. Blanchard looked up at me. "We have protocols for things like this. You were taken off a case and disobeyed orders to leave it alone." I swallowed a lump in my throat. "I have to say, I admire your persistence in acquiring the Bayshire. But I have to ask. Why are you doing this? Especially, when you know the consequences."

I wasn't sure how to respond. What was her angle here? "I'm here to get the stone," I said.

"But why?"

"Ms. Blanchard, I'm a good agent." I paused, trying to piece together what I was going to say. I couldn't mess this up. "When I first went after it, we were ambushed. There is more to this stone than I think we realize. I should be the one to finish the case." I wanted to tell her I thought I was wrongfully taken off the case, that Mr. Martial made an irrational decision, that I deserved to be an instructor. But I couldn't question her, not when my entire career was already at risk.

I held my breath, waiting for her to say something. Anything. She was the big boss. Right now, she controlled my future. Her expression was unreadable as she seemed to contemplate what to say to me. I braced myself for the worst.

"If you want information about the Bayshire Stone, I suggest speaking with Agent Z."

What? Did I hear her correctly? Was she seriously about to help me?

"So, you're not sending me back to Ohio?" I asked.

"I think I can overlook this one thing. Unfortunately, I can't speak for your director. But you can't disobey any more orders, not from Mr. Martial, not from me. I know there's more at stake here for you than you're saying. Do you understand?"

"Yes, Ma'am." Did I? She obviously knew about me being chosen as an instructor. She was part of the decision and head of the Training Camp. But she wasn't punishing me. She was helping.

"Dismissed," Ms. Blanchard said.

Ms. Blanchard was actually letting me go? She had nothing else to say?

It took me a moment to put things together in my head. Agent Z. The Bayshire Stone. Agent Z was Amelia Zegro, my old friend from Training Camp. To think that I came all the way out here to find out my old friend knew about the Bayshire. My thoughts kept me frozen in place.

"Yes, Agent Mills?" Ms. Blanchard asked since I didn't leave. Was she irritated at me? I couldn't tell.

"Where do I find Agent Z?" I asked.

"She's in her office right now. But I need to warn you." Ms. Blanchard became serious. More serious, if that was possible.

I hesitated. "Warn me about what?"

"A little while ago, Agent Z was in a terrible accident."

"Accident?"

"She hasn't been quite herself. She suffered from a severe injury to the head and her memory isn't working properly."

"What do you mean?"

Ms. Blanchard looked me in the eye, and a cold sensation ran through me. "Agent Z is suffering from partial memory loss."

Chapter 18
Memory Loss

My heart sank. Memory loss? That was one of the worst things that could happen to an agent! To anyone. What did that mean for Amelia? She had to be okay. Amelia was always tough, fast on her feet, and quick to think ahead. She was an exceptional agent, even though she was a bit more of a rule follower. If Amelia had amnesia, would she even be able to help me?

Ms. Blanchard rose from her seat and walked around her desk to perch on the corner. "I'm aware that the two of you have a history together from the training camp."

I nodded.

"You and she, along with Agent Steinfeld, were quite the team."

I smiled, excited that Ms. Blanchard recognized our talents all the way back from camp. Emily and Amelia were an amazing team, and I was honored to be their friend. She went on. "You can't mention Agent Steinfeld to Agent Z."

It was like a bomb went off in Headquarters. Everything shook, then it went eerily still. Did I seriously just hear that? I wasn't sure. A fatal punch in the gut. "What?" The two were best friends, inseparable. What happened?

"Agent Z does not remember that Emily is an agent," Ms. Blanchard clarified. I hung to her every word as I made sense of what she was saying. "Due to unfortunate circumstances and precautions, we are keeping this information from Agent Z until she has completed her current case and recovered on her own." I tightened my jaw to keep myself from saying something. How would that make anything better? I didn't dare ask. "Under no circumstances can you unveil this information to her," the Director continued. "Agent Z is one of my best agents here at Headquarters, and I intend to keep it that way. I cannot have her distracted. Do you understand?"

"Yes, Ma'am. May I ask how this happened?"

"I'm afraid that is confidential information."

I nodded, expecting that as her answer. "Thank you, Ms. Blanchard."

I headed back to my quarters in a daze. Memory loss. Wow. I sat on my bunk, wondering what I was supposed to do. How was Amelia dealing with this? How was Emily? It didn't seem reasonable to keep that sort of information in the dark. But I couldn't question the Director's authority. She had to know what was best for her agents.

Would Amelia even remember who I was? My heart ached at the thought of one of my first friends at the T.S.O. not remembering me. It was unthinkable. But when it came down to it, it didn't matter. I needed whatever information she had about the Bayshire Stone. I couldn't lose sight of my mission.

I left my bunk and headed to Agent Z's office.

Chapter 19
Agent Z

I stopped outside Amelia's open office door. I was actually going to see her! After all this time. A sense of dread kept me from stepping into the doorway. What if she didn't remember me? What was I supposed to say? I had never dealt with memory loss. Physical pain I could handle. But how was I supposed to handle this?

I peeked inside. Amelia was staring intently at her computer. She looked different. More mature. Her hair was longer.

"Well, that's upsetting," she said, leaning back in her chair.

I smiled to myself. She hadn't noticed me. Hearing her voice helped me calm down. She was still Amelia. That was enough. I stepped into the doorway. "What's upsetting?"

Amelia startled, jerking in my direction. "Alexis?" A smile quickly replaced the shocked look on her face.

I came in and sat across from her. Relief raised my spirits. She remembered me! I felt myself relax. It was still the same Amelia from camp. She had a simple office, not much more than a desk and two chairs, but nice, and her own private office. It was much nicer than having to share a tiny cubic office space with every other agent at the Ohio T.S.O. base.

"What's up with you lately?" I asked, thinking about everything Ms. Blanchard told me. I couldn't keep my curiosity at bay. "I heard you were in an accident, maybe even some memory loss."

"That's what they tell me." Amelia shrugged her shoulders. "Just working on another case."

"An invisible battle scar, well, we can't all be that lucky." I thought of my fall back at camp, of the now permanent scar on my calf. That was quite the story to explain to Mom and Dad. Let's just say I could no longer go cliff diving. As far as my parents knew, it didn't go well my first time.

"I don't know," Amelia said. "It seems to be causing problems with my current case." I nodded. Especially without Emily. How was Amelia doing this? I admired her calmness with the situation. I knew she wouldn't tell me exactly how she was feeling. "Nothing I can't handle," she said, giving me a smile.

"Now there's the Amelia I remember." She laughed.

"How have you been? I heard you were stationed in Ohio," Amelia said. I could tell she was welcoming my interruption to whatever was upsetting her. I guess I was too.

Now I was getting somewhere. "I'm here on business. Ms. Blanchard said you might have some information for me, about a red diamond. Very important."

"I don't know anything about a red diamond." Amelia thought for a moment, choosing her words carefully. She knew something. "But I did see a picture of one when I was-" she stopped. When she was what? Did she or did she not know about the stone? "I saw a picture of one at a friend's house," she continued. "But how did Ms. Blanchard know that? I haven't given any reports yet."

She could have seen any red rock. Amelia didn't know. For all I knew, it could be some kid's arts and crafts photo of a painted rock. Ms. Blanchard didn't share with me how she knew what she did. But she was the director. How she knew didn't matter. But if Amelia knew anything that would help me get the Bayshire Stone, then I needed her help. Yes, I had a plan. But I was always open to new ideas.

"I don't know, but please let me know if you find out anything else on the rock," I said. "In the wrong hands, it can be quite dangerous." I paused for a moment. How was I going to get the stone by myself? My partner was on the opposite side of the country. Amelia was preoccupied. She couldn't help me, not now. I desperately wanted Tanner with me right now. "We'll have to catch up later before I leave," I said.

"Will do."

I smiled at Amelia, hoping everything worked out for her. "Talk to you later. I've got to get going." I left her office. It was good to see her, but I couldn't help but worry about her. I had no clue what I would do if I suddenly forgot Tanner was my partner. I relied on him as much as I did myself. But I didn't need her info. I knew what I was going to do. I just didn't know how I was going to do it.

Three days left. Three days before I could go after the Bayshire Stone. Three days to decide what to do.

I walked back to my bunk. At least Amelia could be an asset if I needed her. Hopefully.

I stopped and thought for a moment, looking up and down the dank hallway. I still hadn't been outside. I went from the airport, to the subway, to here, not once stepping foot outside in the sunshine. Maybe I needed some fresh air.

In the cafeteria, I found a list of all the above-ground access points to Headquarters posted on the wall. There was a spot in the town park. That would work. I left the cafeteria and headed to the subway.

Deep in thought, I wasn't watching where I was going. Ms. Blanchard stood right in front of me.

"Agent Mills."

"Yes, Ms. Blanchard?" I stumbled backward and regained my balance.

"What information did you discover from Agent Z?" the Director asked.

"Nothing. She's never even heard of the Bayshire."

Ms. Blanchard looked at me expectantly, arms held behind her back. "Anything else?"

"No," I said. Why did she care? She gave me a potential lead. That was awesome, but why did she want to know what I discovered? I didn't know her very well. She was a lot nosier than Mr. Martial. Maybe that's just how Headquarters was run. And I couldn't blame her for being worried about Agent Z.

Ms. Blanchard nodded her head, her lips pursed together in thought. She turned and left.

Chapter 20
You Just Wait

I exited the storage room of the bathroom facility, not the cleanest place. The summer heat hit me like a punching bag. I had forgotten how hot it was in California.

I sat on a bench facing the playground, watching two small boys chase each other through the grass. First I texted my parents, telling them I was okay and making up a story about a field trip to the museum in Houston.

I had to talk to someone about all this. Miles would just start asking me information if I called him, wanting a progress report when I had nothing.

I called Tanner. Tanner would just listen. And I wanted to know what my partner would say. I told him about being followed at the airport, wondering if all of it was just in my head. I told him about the waitress. Tanner listened to me worry about Ms. Blanchard and Amelia. I struggled to keep myself from raising my voice in public.

"Am I going crazy?" I asked. "I…I'm being followed, my friend has memory loss, I've already lost the stone twice." I waved my arm around as I complained. "I'm starting to think I'm not cut out for this case."

"Calm down," Tanner said when I stopped ranting. He didn't sound angry at all. Maybe even amused. "You are not crazy. You're obviously being followed." Like that wasn't obvious. But I knew how to handle keeping my cover. Besides, I was still waiting for the stone to arrive. Headquarters was just about as safe a place to hide out as it could get. I couldn't mess this up.

"What am I supposed to do now?" I asked.

"You just wait," Tanner said, his voice smooth over the phone.

"Really?"

"You can't make big assumptions about the Director. Like you said, we don't know her very well. And as for Agent Z, she's got her own problems to fix. If Miles said it will be there in three days from now, you just have to wait for it to arrive."

"I hate that word." Tanner laughed. Telling me to wait was like forcing a child to eat his broccoli. Tanner knew that, but he was right. He usually was, which is why he's my partner. As much as I didn't want to admit it, waiting was my only option. "I wish you were here," I grumbled into the phone. Then my words hit me. Heat burned my cheeks.

"Really?" Tanner asked. I could tell he was smiling, and I blushed harder. Why did I have to say that?

I scrambled to cover my tracks. He couldn't know that I liked him, not like that. "I mean, I kind of need my partner right now."

"Hey, why is Miles handling all the technical stuff for me?" I asked.

"He said you wanted him to."

"I never said that." I shook my head.

"Either way, I'm in charge of keeping your parents updated about your trip. And when people start asking questions, I'll be here to cover for you at base. Maybe it's better I'm not as involved. For both of our sakes."

"You're probably right." I sighed.

"You're doing fine," Tanner said. But by the sound of his voice, he was probably still smiling. And I bet it was a little wider than usual. If only I could have seen it in person. "I'm keeping your parents busy," he said.

"What are you telling them?"

"I'm sending updates about your trip to make it look like they're from chaperones. If worse comes to worst, you'll have an extended trip and a delayed flight. Don't worry."

"Thanks." At least they wouldn't be totally in the dark. If I called them though, Mom would see right through my lies over the phone. I couldn't let that happen.

"Just keep your head clear and stay focused," Tanner said.` And as always, Tanner was right.

Chapter 21
D32

I spent the next two days training. I went over maps of the museum. I trained in the gym. I looked over every piece of info the T.S.O. had about the museum and the Bayshire Stone. I didn't learn much more about the stone, which was becoming the biggest thorn in my foot right now. I traced and retraced my steps inside the museum until I knew it like my own bedroom. There was no way Mr. Bard or his goons were going to stop me. Not this time.

Finally, the day came. The stone arrived at the Glayfield Earth and Space Museum. I sat in the cafeteria, having just finished my lunch, which I had forced myself to eat. My stomach wouldn't sit still. Miles called me.

"It's being held in storage room D32 on the underground level," he said, going over all the facts I already memorized. "The Bayshire was transferred in a black briefcase. "Each artifact has its own storage room, so it should be the only thing in there. The door is going to be locked."

"Of course they would lock it." Sometimes Miles could be so dense.

"The case requires both a four-digit code and a key to open it," he said.

"No problem. I can use the decoding device and my key card," I said.

Miles continued with his fun facts while I tried to figure out how I could get my hands on another key card to unlock the door. "A few months ago, there was a big robbery," Miles explained. "Jewelry was stolen from the museum."

"Then I go during open hours. There will be more people, and I'll have better cover."

"I doubt it. That place is always guarded, especially since that last robbery. It doesn't matter how many people there are. If you go later tonight, there should be fewer people at the museum. It will be easier to get around."

I wasn't sure about that. Security was bound to be heavier when the museum was closed, but I didn't contradict him. "Sounds good," I said, nodding over the phone. Miles knew what he was talking about, considering he was the expert in logistical tactics. I took him for his word. If only tonight would get here sooner.

I hung up the phone and pulled up the blueprints of the storage facility. Suddenly, Amelia and Emily walked up to me. I shut off my phone.

"We need to talk," Amelia whispered across the table. Both she and Emily looked nervous on the edge of their seats. Emily still looked the same as she did from camp, short blonde hair and rosy cheeks.

"What is it?" I asked. "Why are we whispering?" I suppressed the urge to ask what Amelia remembered, noticing she and Emily came in together. This had to be a sign she was getting better.

"We need your help," Emily said. "We don't want Ms. Blanchard knowing. By the way, it's nice to see you." Emily said.

Amelia remembered who Emily was. They were partners again. And Ms. Blanchard didn't know. Why?

"You said you were here on business. You were looking for some type of stone," Amelia said. "The Bayshire?"

She did know! Or at least she'd found out.

"That's right. And I know exactly where it is." I smiled from ear to ear, unable to hide my excitement. "I discovered the stone is owned by a private investor who collects rare objects from both earth and space. The Bayshire is currently on tour and going on exhibit here at the Glayfield Earth and Space Museum. I was going to retrieve it tonight."

"We have to go after it now," Amelia said, her voice on the verge of breaking. "As in right now."

"Why?"

Emily explained. "Dr. Doom, the guy we're tracking down, is planning on stealing it within the next few hours. We can't let that happen."

There was another person trying to get the Bayshire, too? What was it with this rock?! I couldn't let that happen! I needed to bring the Bayshire back to Ohio. Amelia was right. We couldn't wait for tonight. No one was stealing that stone but me.

The two agents followed me to my bunk. I grabbed a small backpack from the closet, big enough to carry the stone. I put the decoder device inside the bag and stuffed my key card in my pocket. This was happening now.

Chapter 22
Glayfield Earth and Space Museum

The moment we walked into the museum, my phone buzzed. There was a text from Tanner.

Agent W is there.

Shoot. Agent Watson was here? Why? Just to see me mess up? To watch me fail again? I pictured his face when he tried to taunt me after getting taken off the case. I would not let that happen.

"The stone goes on exhibit tomorrow," I said, leading Amelia and Emily to the underground storage facility. It took a lot of effort to control my breathing. Thoughts of Agent W wouldn't leave me alone. He always had to show up at the worst time. Why couldn't he just let me deal with this on my own? Couldn't he quit trying to outdo me at my own cases for once? There was no way he was going to mess this up for me. I was going to make sure of it.

We walked through the main lobby and passed an exhibit about the dawn of time.

Then I saw him.

The same man in the black sweatshirt from the airport was browsing a shelf of books and flyers off to my left. Two things clicked in my head. Number one: The man in the hood stopped twice in the airport and looked at books when he was following me. Number two: Damien was always reading in between classes, during his free time at camp. He couldn't stay away from books even when he was on the job.

The man turned around, pulled down his hood. He moved to an exhibit across the room. The first thing I recognized was the haircut, the shaved off, military-style hair. I stared at him. He was the one that had been following me. I spun around before he spotted me and picked up my pace.

No matter what, I couldn't let Damien get the stone. It didn't matter if he worked for Mr. Bard, the T.S.O., or anyone else. I had to create a diversion.

I pushed my friends through the door that read **Authorized Personnel Only.**

I slammed the door shut behind me and faced Emily and Amelia. Three different passageways extended from where we were standing.

"The stone is in storage locker D32." My heart sank into the pit of my stomach as I realized what I had to do. "It will probably be in a black case with a four-digit code and a key." I handed them my decoding device from inside my backpack, and Emily tucked it inside her own. "Your key card should work just fine for the other part." I looked back at the closed door behind me.

I wanted to get the Bayshire. I wanted it so bad. But Agent Watson was more important right now. It didn't matter who grabbed the stone from the case, as long as I was the one to bring it back home. With Amelia and Emily finding the stone, I could figure out what Damien was up to and how to stop him. It was up to the others to get the Bayshire. "I'll guard the door," I said.

I left and shut the door behind me, leaving Emily and Amelia on their own in the storage area.

Agent Watson wasn't too far away. I walked down the hallway and back out into the open area of the museum.

Damien still hadn't seen me.

I pulled down on my gloves until they hurt and took a deep breath.

"Can I help you?" I asked.

"No, I'm okay." Watson turned around. The moment he recognized me, he sneered, crossing his arms in front of him. "Well, well," he said. I wasn't surprised. He had to know I was on to him. The real question was why he was here. "You know," Watson said, "there have been rumors back at base that Agent Mills went rogue; that she can't do what she's told. Guess they were true." The gleam in his eye made me sick.

"Shut up."

Agent Watson scoffed. I stood firm, not wanting to bring more attention to myself in public. I grabbed him by the arm. "Let's take this somewhere a bit more private." And a bit further away from the Bayshire Stone.

"Ooh, Sorry but, uh, I'm not really interested. I like girls with a bit more flare." Damien looked me up and down. Where the heck did that come from? I wanted to drop a block of cement on his head.

"Oh, you mean like someone who's just as annoying as you are? Good luck finding someone like that." I tugged the sleeve of his sweatshirt and pulled him behind me, resisting the urge to say more. I dragged him into the next room where there weren't any people. He didn't resist, just followed behind me. I let go of him and turned to face him. I balled my fists, readying myself if he decided he wanted to fight instead of talk.

84

"I'm here on business, Agent Mills," Damien said.

"Really?" Talking it is then.

"When they took you off the case, it still had to be finished." Based on his tone, I wasn't sure whether he was talking about the Bayshire case or something else. Was he trying to take my place as an instructor too? "I was more than happy to take the job." He teased. "No task force team necessary."

That's it. I couldn't take it. Before I could stop myself, my clenched fist hit him in the jaw. He came all the way here to get the Bayshire. Lucky for me, that was already being taken care of. Damien wiped the blood from his lip, laughing. He had such a nerve.

"This is my case," I said.

"Whatever you say." He smiled, the small line of blood from the corner of his lips making it even more repulsive.

"Just stay out of my way," I said. I turned away from him, not caring if I won that fight. Finishing this case was more important than settling scores with people who couldn't be reasoned with. Mr. Martial really had to hate me to send Watson on my case instead of any other possible person in the T.S.O. It was more annoying than Mr. Bard. Now that I thought of it, I hadn't seen Mr. Bard or his henchmen at all since entering California. What if Amelia and Emily ran into them? I had to get back to them.

As soon as I was out of Mr. Perfect's view, I broke into a run. Hopefully he had the sense not to follow. Just as I arrived at the door where I left Amelia and Emily, it swung open.

"Did you get it?" I asked, hoping they didn't notice I left.

"It's in the bag." Emily said, nodding towards her backpack.

"Alright. Let's get out of here."

85

I walked quicker through the museum than I probably should have. Amelia was watching me. It was difficult to ignore her worried gaze. "You okay?" she asked.

"Just peachy," I said with a fake smile. I kept my eyes open for anyone who had the nerve to get in my way.

As we got to the front doors, I spotted Damien again. He glared at me with pure hatred as he watched me leave. He stood beside a giant map of the museum, fists clenched. I gave him a smug look. He knew he lost.

"What is it?" Amelia asked, noticing I stopped walking.

"Nothing. Let's get out of here." We stopped outside near the bike rack. "I can take the Bayshire into Headquarters. It will be safer there."

"Good idea," Emily said. She took the stone out of her backpack and I gently placed it in mine.

With a quick wave, we parted ways. I watched from around the corner, holding onto my bike, as Agent Watson came through the doors.

He looked so angry, his eyes narrowed, arms tight by his side. Did he still go to the storage area? Did he try to find the Bayshire after we left? He walked towards Emily and Amelia. I held my breath. Would he try to take the stone from them, thinking they had it? He couldn't have known they were agents. I tightened my grip on the backpack. Agent Watson bumped into Amelia's shoulder and kept walking. Did he really have to rub it in like that? He was so immature, so selfish.

I hopped on my bike and rode towards the nearest access point to headquarters. Something new was bothering me. I knew how to keep my cover. The only reason I was being followed by Mr. Perfect was because he knew my tricks. He had the same training, so my attempts to hide did nothing since he was going to the same place. And I was right about their being hardly any security at the museum. If they had sent Watson after the stone, maybe there was less security for a reason. The T.S.O. had a way of making that happen when we needed it to. Despite how beside myself I was with him stealing my case, maybe it was a good thing. He made it a little easier for me. In a way. Maybe.

Unlike what I told Amelia and Emily, the stone was going in my bunk. There was no way I would put it in the T.S.O. Safe. Especially not with Damien walking around. Not until I got to Ohio.

Chapter 23
Dr. Doom

I stuffed everything into my duffel bag, including the Bayshire Stone.

Instead of a plane ride, Miles got me a ticket for a train all the way back to Ohio. It was safer to transport the Bayshire by train. If it started freaking out, it would be safer for everyone to have it on the ground than in the air inside a giant electrical machine. Planes crashed when they slowed down. Trains were my best bet.

I was relieved we didn't run into Mr. Bard yesterday, or any of his so-called security guards. But the fact that getting the stone was so easy sent chills down my spine. If he wasn't there, he had to be somewhere. And not knowing was worse.

Amelia and Emily explained what had happened in the storage room. It was just by luck they had picked the right case, since there were multiple ones in the room. I guess Miles didn't know everything. But there wasn't any extra security or guards at all. I had the stone. I got Agent Watson to bleed, if only a little. It had been a good day.

Now it was late in the afternoon, and I was itching to get back home. I had a few hours left before I needed to leave. Just like the airport, the subway led to the train station. If only the T.S.O. subway traveled throughout the country. Unfortunately, it didn't.

My phone started buzzing. It was Emily.

"Do you think you could help us tonight?" she asked.

"Help you with what?"

"Dr. Doom is attempting a prison break tonight. Amelia and I are going after him. You up for that?"

The Bayshire needed to get back to Ohio, before Agent Watson figured out where it was. He had to be in Headquarters somewhere. But they did help me get the stone. It was the least I could do to return the favor. Besides, it would be nice to help catch a criminal. And what if I didn't go? Amelia was still dealing with an injury. If I said no, they could get hurt. An image of Tanner and his boot flashed through my mind.

And then there were my parents. I couldn't imagine how mad my parents must be right now. I pictured Dad sitting in the living room, his face red with anger while Mom paced back and forth, wringing her hands together. They had already lost one daughter. They must be terrified at the thought of losing another. Maybe I should have answered their constant phone calls. But I wouldn't have known what to say. My lies wouldn't be enough for them.

"Alexis?"

I sighed, stomping my foot on the ground. I couldn't believe I was going to do this, but I couldn't bring myself to say no. If something happened to my friends and I wasn't there, I would never forgive myself. Hailey would have said yes. "Sure. I'm in." Emily gave me her address and explained to me what Doom was planning.

This man was going to break his brother out of jail. She also explained to me why Amelia was so set on getting him. Dr. Doom put her in the hospital. It was this guy who took her memory! Just that fact alone made me despise the man.

I hid the stone in the closet before I left. The last thing I needed was having it stolen from me. I looked back in my bunk from the doorway, telling myself it would be okay. Who would break into Headquarters, anyway? It had to be okay to leave the stone for a little while longer, to help my friends.

I grabbed one of the T.S.O. bikes and rode to Emily's place. When I got to her house, she equipped me with a pair of night-vision goggles. I strapped them to my belt.

I followed behind Amelia and Emily. Neither of them spoke. We stopped at an ice cream parlor near the bus stop, where they explained the plan to me.

They were going to wait until closing time, then attempt to arrest Dr. Doom in the Electrical Room, where he planned to shut down the security system. I thought of the Bayshire, of the explosion I learned about at the exhibit in Texas. It was good this Dr. Doom wouldn't be using it. I tried not to picture what would happen if he did. It would have been much worse.

Dr. Doom was planning to break out his brother, the father of one of Amelia's friends. Her name was Savannah. Emily pointed to a cell block on the blueprints. An X was drawn over top of it. She believed this was where Doom's brother was. There was one thing that didn't make sense.

"What about this one?" I pointed to another cell, one that was circled.

"I'm not sure. It's in a completely different part of the building." Amelia shook her head. She didn't know what to do. She pointed to the hallways that stretched through the complex like a maze. "We've got to stop him there before he opens the cell."

I was ready for a fight. Aside from Agent Watson, there hadn't been a lot of butt-kicking since Texas, if that even counted. I wanted to feel my blood running through my veins like I did back on cases in Ohio. I wanted the rush of the fight. Maybe this was what I needed.

We boarded a city bus and made it to the prison. After riding on the bus as far as Amelia and Emily planned, we rode our bikes the rest of the way, stopping in front of a huge fence that wrapped around the entire facility.

"Should we use the grappling hook?" Emily asked, staring up at the giant fence in front of us. I thought they would have figured out how to get into the facility already. Oh well. The fence was at least twenty feet high, with barbed wire strung at the top. I stepped away from the other agents for a moment and took in my surroundings.

We were in the parking lot. A small group of people was heading towards the gate entrance. Bam. "No need," I said, answering Emily's question about the grappling hook.

We snuck in with the group of people and slid past the security gate. I followed Emily and Amelia, ready to help in whatever way needed. The faster we were done, the faster I could get back home. The thought of the Bayshire just sitting in my bunk waiting to be grabbed was unsettling.

We waited for visiting hours to end, then crouched outside between the bushes on the side of the building. I glanced at Amelia. She crouched beside me, her eyes focused in front of her. Her plan was pretty sound, but she didn't plan an escape if one was necessary. I couldn't let her get hurt any further.

After a few minutes, a tall man approached the entrance. He put a ski mask over his head and pulled out a weapon I had never seen before, blasting the door to pieces with it. The sound of a gun went off in my head again, the same one that shot my sister. I waved dust away from my face and opened my eyes. I was shaking in my boots. I hated guns. If you must fight, use your hands. I considered a gun cheating in the cruelest way possible. Dust floated to the ground. That was definitely Dr. Doom.

Chapter 24
We Catch a Traitor

The ringing in my ears from Doom's gun faded. Among the chaos, we raced back towards the gate. Amelia found the controls inside the guard shack and let Savannah in. The girl looked different from what I imagined. She was quiet and reserved based on her shy attitude and nervous expression towards me.

Emily walked around the gate in search of the missing guards. She came back, her cheeks flushed. "They're lying against the gate on the other side, up against the post's wall," she said.

"That sounds comfortable," I grumbled.

"Come on," Amelia said. "We need to hurry."

I glanced at the gate, then at Savannah. Amelia had told me before that Savannah was supposed to help her uncle, Dr. Doom, from inside a van. "Wait a moment," I said. I narrowed my eyes at Savannah. "If you're not in the van, won't Doom realize that?"

"Yeah," Emily said, catching on. Was Savannah actually on their side? After being chased the entire way across the country, I didn't want to take any more chances.

"He was just going to have me give him directions," Savannah said, her voice shaking. "Since the lights were going to be off. I made a recording. It's playing into his earpiece." Well, it was good enough for me. And frankly, I was too tired of messing up to find a reason for her to lie.

We rushed back to the prison entrance and inside the visiting center. The floor was littered with pieces of wood and glass from the door. Chairs were strewn across the room. The guard at the desk was tied up.

This Dr. Doom took out a door with a single blast from his gun. He meant business. I failed to calm myself and tugged on my gloves to keep my blood flowing. The gunshot that killed my sister played through my head. It was like I was ten years old again.

The man who shot my sister flashed through my mind. I pushed the memory aside. I had to focus. I shook my head, hyping myself up. This man wanted the Bayshire Stone for this. It was all connected. This was becoming more complicated than I thought it would be.

Inside the visitor center, we found a guard tied up at his desk. Amelia unlocked the guard's handcuffs. "Where do the doors lead?" she asked once the guard was paying attention.

"Who are you kids?" He rubbed feeling back into his wrists. I rolled my eyes. Why was it such a mystery who we were? Okay, I get it. It was strange, a bunch of teens in a prison after visiting hours, but we just rescued him for crying out loud! Give us some credit.

"Special agents of the T.S.O.," Amelia said. "How do I get to the control room?"

After a long and pointless explanation that I didn't pay much attention to, the man pulled up the security feed.

On the monitor, we saw a man in a ski mask in the Electrical Room. My blood raced as my heart pounded in my chest. This was going to be fun.

The security feed turned to static. "That guy on the camera is trying to break someone out of your prison," Amelia explained. The urgency in her tone kept me on my feet.

After a moment that felt like forever, the guard guided us to the Electrical Room. Dr. Doom was working at a computer terminal. I smiled at the ski mask. It was such a cheesy disguise. Mine would have been a hundred times better, even though Tanner would disagree.

"Put your hands on your head!" the guard shouted, running to Doom and forcing his hands behind his back. I kept myself from lunging at the constrained man. This was still Agent Z's case. "You have the right to remain silent," the officer continued. "Anything you say can and will be used against you."

I stayed near the door, not wanting to interfere unless I had to. Amelia pulled off Doom's mask.

"I thought he was here!" Savannah said in dismay. Amelia and Emily shared a worried glance. Now I was confused. Was that not Doom? I was missing something big.

"He knew the guard would check the control room, so he sent someone else to do that part." Amelia slammed her hand down on the table. "I should have known he wouldn't just walk in here!"

So it wasn't Doom. I stepped into the room and inspected the man. Now I could see his face. And I recognized him.

"I know you!" I shouted. "I saw you when I first arrived at Headquarters! On the subway." I glared at the man. "You're the new computer technician. You just joined the T.S.O." I laughed. "I should have known something was up when I first met you."

The man snickered at me. I balled my fists. It was actually the man from the subway. I skimmed my memory for his name. He said it at the check-in center. Mr. O'Neil. Mind. Blown.

"Do you act alone within the T.S.O.?" Emily asked.

The man laughed. "I get my orders from someone deep within the T.S.O."

"Who is it?" Amelia demanded.

I was trying to wrap my head around the idea of a traitor inside the organization. The thought already crossed my mind with Watson, but now I was actually facing a real traitor. I was dealing with enough already.

"You will never find out, Agent Z. My loyalty goes far beyond Dr. Doom." Mr. O'Neil continued laughing. I resisted the urge to mess up his face.

"Come on, I think I know where he is," Amelia said, shoving the man in the guard's direction. I followed Agent Z outside towards the cell block.

Chapter 25
Nothing but Lies

My mind was spinning. There was a traitor in the organization. Were there others? Whatever was going on would not end well.

We crept inside the building through an opened side door. It was pitch black. My years of training kicked in, automatically turning on stealth-mode. I grabbed the night vision goggles from my belt and forced myself to walk lighter on my feet. Through the goggles, I could make out the dark hallways, cell after cell on either side of us. Savannah was close enough I could hear her short breaths. Emily pulled on her goggles.

"Stay close," Amelia whispered, her words slicing through the air like arrows. We followed her down the hallway, step after step on the cement floor.

Twenty feet in front of us, a man was kneeling down beside a security guard. My mind flashed to the ambush back at the penthouse in Ohio. This time I couldn't mess up. The security guard in front of me was innocent. People were already hurt. I wasn't going to lose this time.

This man was definitely Dr. Doom. There was no way I was wrong.

Emily and Amelia rushed ahead. I grabbed Savannah's hand, feeling it tremble in mine. This had to be hard for her. Together Savannah and I walked down the hallway, not saying a word. If only there was a way to comfort a total stranger. Savannah didn't have goggles. She was blind in here. I couldn't do anything but grasp her trembling hand and guide her through the prison. We traced Amelia's steps, staying close so I could see her without getting in the way.

I wanted to hit someone. I wanted to take charge, run down the hall, and pounce on Dr. Doom. He was too much like the men who killed my sister. He relied on his weapons. He was weak. But this wasn't my case. I needed to be the supporter right now, not the leader. I balled up my energy and forced it to wait until I could release it.

Shouting and banging erupted from all sides. Savannah's grip got tighter as my ears rang from the increased noise. It was all the inmates, shouting in their cells. The tension in the room was just about to blow the cell doors from their hinges.

The lights on the ceiling turned back on. I pulled off my goggles and strapped them to my belt. Amelia, Emily, and Dr. Doom were not in front of us. I lost them.

"Let's go," I said to Savannah, letting go of her hand. I rushed down the hall, turning the corner into another section of the building.

Doom was in front of me, lying on the floor. Amelia lay beside him, panting. Emily was pulling herself up on the other side of Doom, blood smeared on her chin.

I raced toward the fight. I jumped on top of Dr. Doom and held him in place. Amelia pulled herself off the ground. She and Emily grabbed his arms. We trapped him. Dr. Doom continued to kick, jostling me every which way. He was like a human bull, but I stayed on.

The three of us rolled the man onto his stomach. I sat on top of him, grabbing a pair of cuffs from my belt and securing them on his wrists.

"There's no point in struggling," Amelia said. "What's this?" she pulled a pair of keys out of his pocket. "Ahh, this is what you took from that guard. Nice try." A grin spread across my face.

I missed teaming up with Agent Z and Agent Steinfeld. Sure. I took people down all the time with Tanner and trained with Miles every week. But these were my girls. It was different now, different compared to working with the guys back at base.

The sound of a door bursting open pulled me from my thoughts. A group of men, all in uniform, were heading straight toward us.

"Quiet down!" one man shouted. Slowly the buzz in my ears faded, and the shouting became a whisper. "The name's Captain Wilson," he said as he shook Amelia's hand. I would have greeted him, but my seat on top of Doom was becoming quite comfortable.

Amelia explained what happened to the captain. We were agents of the T.S.O. The guy I was sitting on was Mr. Jason, or Dr. Doom. I bent over so Doom could see me and waved. He glared back, still trying to make me lose my balance. He didn't know how stubborn I was. Foolish man. That wasn't going to happen.

After a few minutes Amelia and Savannah walked down the corridor, an officer in front of them. They were going to the cell that was marked on the blueprints to see Savannah's dad.

"You can get off him now, miss," an officer said to me. I grabbed Doom's cuffed wrists as I climbed off his back and hauled him to his feet. Captain Wilson took him from me. I brushed off my pants. Emily smiled at me, holding her bleeding jaw with her hand.

"Sir," Emily started. "This man has caused a lot of harm. Aside from breaking into your prison, he is also a jewelry thief. He could probably be charged for child abuse too considering what he did to Savannah. He could also be charged with possession of an illegal weapon and the attempted murder of Agent Z."

"Is that right?" The captain frowned at Doom. Wilson's jaw was square and his face was wrinkled from age and smiling. His hair was white. "We're going to have some fun here, aren't we?" he asked. I liked him.

Amelia and Savannah returned. Amelia walked up to Mr. Jason and slapped him across the face. I flinched. When did Amelia get so violent?

"Do you understand what you put your niece through?" Amelia asked. Her face and ears were red. I'd never seen her so angry. Of course, she'd been through a lot since I last saw her. I knew first-hand what trauma could do to a person. I couldn't blame her, but it caught me off guard.

"We explained everything to the captain," I told her.

"He lied to Savannah." Amelia wasn't paying attention to me. "He was never here for her dad. He was here to break out Mr. Kathman, his old partner. He probably even framed Mr. Bakers as well."

Okay. Now that was cold.

"We will definitely look into it, Agent Z," the Captain said, holding Doom back before Amelia could hit him again.

Leaving Dr. Doom in the care of the police, we left the prison and rode our bikes back towards Emily's house. Attempting to clear my head was pointless, so I stayed quiet and listened to Amelia and Emily talk.

100

"I overheard Ms. Blanchard telling you they caught the guy you were fighting, who put you in the hospital," Emily said. I listened more closely, thinking about my own encounter with Director Blanchard. "Since it wasn't Dr. Doom but Mr. Kathman, why did she lie?" Emily asked.

"I'm not sure. Maybe she thought it was him," Amelia said. She was much calmer now.

At least I wasn't the only one who thought Ms. Blanchard's actions were curious. I thought of the way the Director handled my disobeying orders. She just let it go. And how she questioned me about what Amelia knew. Should I tell the girls about it? No. Amelia was worried enough about what was going on in her life. I didn't need to add my problems and concerns to the mix.

"We'll have to look into that later," Amelia finished.

We definitely would. I knew I disobeyed orders by coming after the stone. At least Agent Watson wouldn't get the credit. But the way Ms. Blanchard handled it still shocked me, helping me instead of punishing me or sending me back to Ohio. An unnerving thought hit me. Would she use my actions as leverage to keep me from becoming the Defense Tactics Instructor? She was in charge of Training Camp, after all. She played a huge role in choosing the instructors.

We arrived at Emily's house, where the girls insisted I stay the night. I didn't want to. I couldn't leave the stone alone any longer. Who knows if it was even still there?

"I shouldn't," I said.

"Please?" Emily begged. "It's been forever since we saw each other." I kicked myself for giving in, but saying no could raise too much suspicion.

I texted Miles, having him rebook my train for the next day.

Chapter 26
All Aboard

I woke early in the morning and left before the others were up. Hopefully they wouldn't mind, but I didn't want to have to say goodbye. Besides, I couldn't leave the stone alone any longer. I hadn't been able to sleep, wondering if it was still safe in my bunk.

Using the same access point at the park, I took the subway to Headquarters. I hurried to my room, pulled my bag from the closet, and ripped it open. My duffle bag was still packed the way I left it the day before. The Bayshire Stone was still there! Relief washed over me.

I could get back on track now. The Bayshire needed to get back to Ohio, and I was going to be the one to get it there.

I took a quick shower and changed my clothes. The Bayshire was safe in my bag and I was ready to go. I slung my duffle bag over my shoulder and headed to the subway.

There were voices coming from inside Ms. Blanchard's office. I thought about the conversation on the way home from the prison. Leaning against the door, I listened as quietly as I could.

"Savannah will join the Teen Spy Organization. That way I can keep a closer eye on her. I don't want her getting caught up with the wrong people." There was a pause. What was I listening to? "Agent Mills is heading back to Ohio soon," the Director continued. "I'm not sure if she has it. She doesn't know, but we could use her. We need all the help we can get, before someone else has the same idea." She was talking about me! The tone in Ms. Blanchard's voice was cold and unnerving. "I'm well aware of that. Look, the T.S.O. is not meant to be public knowledge."

I froze. What was going on? I thought of all the suspicions that were building up. Emily and Amelia definitely had a right to be concerned, and so did I. My grip tightened around the strap of my bag, and I ran through the grey hallways to the subway before someone spotted me. I couldn't tell anyone what I heard. No one would believe me, except maybe Amelia and Emily, or maybe Tanner. I wasn't even sure what I heard. The last thing I needed was to be a target on the Director's radar.

I sat on the subway, my breathing heavy. I had disobeyed orders, been followed across the country, dealt with a whack-job criminal, and now I had eavesdropped on the Director of Headquarters! Could I get in more trouble?

Looking down at my bag, the story about the Bayshire from the Texas museum took over my thoughts. How had the stone blown up an MRI machine? Here I was with the very thing that had caused all my problems in the first place. I had actually gotten the stone! That was the most important thing.

Now that I had it, no one was going to take the Bayshire Stone from me! Not again.

The subway platform took me into a storage closet inside the station. What was it with the T.S.O. and storage closets? The tube-like elevator landed, and I walked out into the lobby of the train station. There were lots of chairs for people to wait. There were vending machines and bathrooms off to the left. Three people worked at the desk, where a giant screen on the wall above them displayed the current destinations.

Because I had missed the train yesterday, I no longer had a single trip. Miles could only do so much for me. Miles scheduled me to take a train to Oklahoma, where I would board another one that would take me all the way to Ohio. Either way, it was still safer than traveling by air.

I went up to the desk and purchased my ticket. I still had twenty minutes to wait before my departure. Impatience was becoming my only companion. With a chocolate bar from a vending machine in my hand, I logged into the T.S.O. database on my phone, found Amelia's personal number, and made a call. I needed to say goodbye, to tell her thank you.

After the second ring, she picked up.

"Amelia? It's Alexis. I wanted you to know that I'm heading back to Ohio. The Bayshire Stone is safe in my care, and it looks like your job is done too." I looked around the waiting area as I spoke. I almost dropped my chocolate.

There was the sweatshirt, the buzz-cut hair. Agent Watson was here.

"Thanks, Alexis. Your help was greatly appreciated. Will I be seeing you anytime soon?" Amelia asked, but I wasn't paying much attention anymore.

"Afraid not." I stood up and headed over to the restrooms, where it would be harder for Watson to see me. Why did I call her at the worst time?

"Well, you take care of yourself then," Amelia said.

"You too. I'll call you later." I hung up the phone and threw the chocolate wrapper in the trash. I took off my leather jacket and tucked it away. Damien would recognize it immediately. If only I still had the blonde wig from Texas, it would have been useful. When it came to disguises, changing your outfit or accessories was usually the most practical option.

Inside the bathroom, I pulled out a makeup pallete. Time for a disguise. If Damien saw me, he would take the stone. The fact that he was here and not on a plane meant he already knew I had it and where I was.

I pulled out a pair of hazel eye contacts and put them on. That's a start. My brown eyes disappeared under the green lenses. I took out my ponytail and brushed out the knots in my hair, pinning part of it back with a clip. With the makeup pallete, I applied eyeshadow and some lipstick. Then I used one of my favorite gadgets from the T.S.O. With a little bit of spray, I made my olive skin look darker, my cheeks fuller, and my jawline less sharp.

I looked at myself in the mirror. Alexis Mills was going to have to disappear. I looked down at my hands. Along with my leather jacket, the fingerless gloves were my signature uniform. I ripped off my gloves and stuffed them in my bag. My bag. For the second time on this trip, I found the hidden button that would change the color of my bag. Instead of purple or black, my duffle bag was now a rainbow of colors.

Looking in the mirror was someone slightly different. It was a decent disguise. It was all I had time for.

The train was here. It would have to do.

Chapter 27
Undercover has no Cover

I found my seat near the back of the car. With my duffle bag next to the window, I leaned back on the blue-grey headrest, telling myself to calm down. I studied the entire car, memorizing my exits and how many people were in here. None of them were Mr. Perfect. I felt trapped, but at least I was on the ground.

The train pulled out of the station. What would my parents think of me right now? I'd been ignoring their calls, and it was bothering me. But I couldn't bring myself to call them. Did they still think I was in Texas? Them being super worried was a colossal understatement. It would be difficult explaining to them why I was away longer. If only Texas went as planned.

With music blasting in my ears I tried to relax, but my constant questions wouldn't let me. Was Agent Watson on the train? I thought of Mr. Bard. Where was he now? Not back in Texas, I was sure of it. He has to know the Bayshire was missing. How was he handling that? Why wasn't there any trouble at the museum? I imagined Mr. Bard crying in a corner of his perfect penthouse. It was a good thought.

Why was I so nervous? I had the stone and was on my way back home. I had won. My mission was almost complete. So why couldn't I relax?

But even with my constant worries, my need for sleep took over. I slept for the first nine hours on the train. I didn't think I was that tired. When I woke up, they were serving dinner. I checked my bag. The stone was still inside.

After the dishes were removed from my area, I got nervous. My stomach was turning, and my heart was pounding in my chest. I missed my parents. I missed my bedroom, my friends. Why did I feel homesick now? Mom and Dad would be furious. No, more than furious. That much I knew for sure. What was I going to tell them?

I grabbed my bag and headed to the bathroom. My makeup was still intact. Unfortunately, my mind wasn't. When I opened the bathroom door, I froze. My stomach did a backward flip off the edge of the Grand Canyon.

Agent Watson stood right in front of me.

I smiled and gazed at the floor as I slid past him. He didn't recognize me. Heck, he'd hardly looked at me. When I was back in my seat, I let myself breathe again, sliding deeper into the chair. But it didn't last long.

Agent Watson walked past. He looked at me for a moment. He was deciding whether he knew me. He kept walking. I clutched my bag to my chest and leaned against the window.

Agent Watson slid into the seat beside me. I cringed. So much for the disguise. I glared at him, not saying a word.

"Give it to me," he said, looking at the chair in front of him. If I didn't know better, I would have said his eyes were glowing with the rage that was emanating off of him.

"Give what to you?" I asked.

"I know you have it." Watson glared at me. His eyes showed nothing but anger. Yep, they were on fire.

"No, I don't," I said, flicking my hair back. Agent Watson raised an eyebrow. "I left the rock at Headquarters. It was too dangerous to travel with." I looked away from him as his eyes continued to glare at me. "It's safe there."

"Quit with the games, Mills. This is my case now."

"I wouldn't give it to you even if I had it." I wondered for a moment why we hated each other. It didn't end with our constant arguments at camp. It should have.

We were in advanced training back at the Ohio base. There was a big test. A competition that took us all over town. Whoever completed the test correctly would be moved to level two of training. They would get to begin their experience in the field, shadowing professional agents. I had wanted it so badly.

Tanner found the map for the competition on the database. We knew where certain points in the competition were and what locations were traps. We flew through the course easily.

Damien figured out what we did afterwards. He just couldn't face the fact I had completed the course before him. When he brought it to Mr. Martial, he credited us for thinking outside the box and using all possible resources. Sure, we cheated, but no one called it that.

It made Damien even angrier with me. If that was even possible.

"It's a nice disguise, you know. But not good enough," he said.

"Gee, thanks for the compliment." Sarcasm dripped from my lips.

"Don't make me do this. I don't want to make a scene."

I looked Agent Watson in the eyes. "Then don't." I wanted him to leave me alone. But I was ready for him to lash out. I was ready to take him. Damien was a good guy. He just had his head screwed on a little too tight.

Agent Watson grabbed me by the collar of my shirt, preventing me from moving away. He breathed down my neck.

"I suggest you leave me alone, Watson." I pried his fingers away from my shirt. "Unless you want that sweatshirt of yours to get messed up."

"You better watch yourself. When this train stops, I'll be leaving with that stone." Agent Watson stood and walked down the aisle. I smoothed down my shirt and took a deep breath. Why was Damien so rude?

But he left himself open. He made himself and his intentions known to me. That was a mistake. Now I knew he was coming. I knew to look out for him. He no longer had the element of surprise.

Chapter 28
Brass Knuckles

With the sound of friction, metal against metal on the tracks, the train came to a stop. I grabbed my bag and muddled in with the crowd. There was a five-minute wait until the next train came.

I purchased my ticket and took a seat at a bench outside.

Where was Agent Watson? My eyes kept darting back and forth, trying to spot the annoying agent. Instead of Mr. Perfect, someone else came into my view. Someone I disliked even more.

Randall Bard.

The man stood on the other side of the platform. Was he on my train? Was he in a different car? I prayed he wouldn't recognize me. He couldn't know I had the stone.

A woman came and sat beside me. She wore dark sunglasses. Her black hair was braided behind her. She had brass knuckles on her fingers. The same ring Mr. Bard's security guards wore back at his penthouse. They were on to me. So much for not being seen.

I stood up and walked around the building towards the parking lot. The sound of footsteps followed. I picked up my pace. In the parking lot, I stuffed my duffel bag into a trash can. Worst-case scenario, Agent Watson finds it and brings it back. As long as Mr. Bard didn't find it. I cringed at the thought.

The woman approached with three men running behind her. I recognized one of them from Mr. Bard's penthouse.

"Mr. Bard would like what belongs to him," the woman said. She glared at me as she approached.

"Well, tell Mr. Bard he can't have it!"

The three goons charged forward. I grabbed the woman's arm and shoulder, flipping her behind me. One man threw a punch. I caught it right in the jaw.

My blood was racing with adrenaline. I spun and kicked the other man in the stomach. He buckled over as he stumbled backwards. The man who hit me in the face caught my arm from behind, jamming his elbow into my shoulder blade. With a shriek, I bent forward. With my free hand, I slipped my acid pen out of my belt and stabbed his arm with it. It only left a tiny dot on his skin. A tiny dot that was burning red and blistering. The man growled, and his arm slacked. I grabbed his arm from behind me and sent him rolling on top of me.

We both crashed to the pavement.

Grunting, I pulled myself to my feet, the pen still in my hand. The man was lying on his back in a crumpled position, grabbing at his arm. But the other man was not. He charged me. "You don't understand what he's doing," I said as I blocked a punch. "He's using you. He doesn't understand how dangerous the stone is."

I ducked down as the man swung a leg in my direction. It passed over my head and connected with my fist.

111

The pen flew from my hand. I held back a shriek as my hand throbbed.

"It's not my job to worry about Mr. Bard's reasons," the man said.

I spun myself around and knocked his foot out from under him. Instead of falling to the ground, he did a backflip and landed on his feet.

"Impressive," I said once we were face to face. He stood in front of me, not making a move. What was he waiting for?

A sharp kick to my left calf sent me falling to my knees on the blacktop.

"Not as impressive as knowing the opponent's weakness and exposing it."

The woman stood behind me, clutching her side. She kicked me in the calf, again. She knew about my injury from the rock wall. How?

Through blurred vision I watched the woman pace around the parking lot, try to open locked cars, and look in the bushes before coming back to her partner.

"She disposed of the bag somewhere," the woman said.

I tried to stand up, but my leg buckled under me. I held my breath as a sharp pain shot through my leg.

"Let's go!" the woman shouted. She grabbed her partner and hauled him off the ground. I gritted my teeth, watching them head back to the station while I knelt on the ground in pain.

"Come on," I said, regretting that it came out as a groan. I couldn't stand up. My leg was failing me.

Chapter 29
Friend or Foe?

I thought I was healed.

"Get up, Mills," a voice said into my ear. Agent Watson crouched beside me. All the muscles in my face tightened as Damien grabbed my arm and pulled me to my feet. It took more effort to stand than it should have.

I shoved him off me. "Thanks."

Damien smirked as he watched me walk past him. Why was he helping me? "You know, there's one thing that they did wrong." I walked towards the trash can, limping painfully. I bit my lip. My fall back at camp was a lot more serious than I wished.

"And what was that?" Damien asked.

"They didn't even try to pry information out of me." I grunted as I pulled off the trash can lid. "They didn't look for what they really wanted." I pulled out my bag, slinging it around my arm. I limped as I turned to face Damien. Embarrassing. Absolutely embarrassing. "I'm taking this into Headquarters and you will not stop me," I said. "I don't need your help, either."

"Really? From the looks of it you couldn't even pull yourself to your feet." Damien raised his voice. He paused, making a "humph" sound. "You know what? You are so self-absorbed!"

"And you're not?"

"I only helped you because you're technically my ally, alright? Any agent of the T.S.O. will always get my help. But you can't just let me have this one, can you? You always have to be in the spotlight."

"I messed up, okay?" I shouted at him, all my anger and guilt rising like bile in my throat. I couldn't hold it in anymore. "They took me off the case. I lost the one position I've wanted forever. It humiliated me!" My heart was racing now. There was blood on my chin from the metal in the man's punch and my leg was ready to give way, but I stood my ground.

When I thought about it, we weren't that different. Maybe that's why we didn't get along. But it didn't matter how much I hated him or vice versa. He was a loyal agent. That much I knew for sure. I could still trust him. And right now, I needed someone to trust.

"I've been followed across the country, Damien. Mr. Martial doesn't trust me, and my entire job is at stake here. I can't even think straight anymore," I said. Damien sighed, but I knew he was listening. Why was I telling him this? That's it. I've officially lost it. I paused, unsure if I could keep going, if it was safe to say anything else. But my anger got the better of me, and I was desperate to have an ally.

"Someone is working inside the T.S.O., back in California," I said. "I came across a double agent when helping my friends. Everywhere I go, someone is out to get me." I shook my head and sighed. I didn't even have a point to this anymore. I was just complaining, and it was getting me nowhere. "Mr. Martial should never have removed me from this case. And I should have fought better. We all make mistakes. You know that." Why was I telling him any of this?

Damien glared at me. "I'm sorry about what happened, Alexis." He paused, staring intensely at his shoes. Did he actually feel sorry for me? That was a first. "If someone is working on the inside of the organization, we need to do something about it. But if you take that stone into Headquarters, it will be me who looks like the fool. I can't fail my case either."

I sighed, looking away from Damien. He would hate me even more if I did that. What was worse was I understood where he was coming from, more than I wanted to. He wasn't a double agent. Damien was never that good of an actor, so he wasn't lying either. There was a moment of silence. I thought about what to do.

If only I wasn't taken off the case in the first place. If I brought the stone in on my own, I could get in trouble for interfering in another agent's case. That wouldn't end well. If I gave him the stone, my entire trip was for nothing. I wouldn't have finished the job, and it wouldn't matter if Mr. Martial knew that or not. I would know, and I was tired of messing up, tired of seeing others suffer because of my actions. Neither of us could go in empty-handed.

I only had one option.

"We take it in together."

Watson raised an eyebrow. "Take it in together, as a team. You and me?" He pointed at each of us.

I rolled my eyes. Was it that difficult to think about us being a team? I guess it was. "Yes, you and me."

"And we both get credit? Both get what we want?"

I nodded.

Agent Watson thought for a moment, then nodded. "It's settled then."

The train whistle blew. Together Agent Watson and I ran back towards the train. It was inching away from the station.

I jumped off the platform and onto the tracks, ignoring the stabbing pain in my leg, forcing myself not to limp. The last car on the train had an open platform, like a balcony. Agent Watson shot ahead of me. The train hadn't started moving fast yet.

Watson pulled himself over the rail and into the back of the train car.

"Let's go!" he shouted to me. I forced my legs to move faster, slowly forcing myself to stop limping. I was gasping for breath from running as I grabbed the rail and pulled myself over the steps. "You need to increase your muscles around your injury," Damien said. He had no expression on his face. I rolled my eyes at him and stepped inside the train car.

I took a window seat and fell backwards into it, resting my head on the soft fabric. My leg was killing me.

Watson sat right behind me.

We almost missed the train. It was Mr. Bard's fault, him and his evil security guards.

Opening up my duffel bag, I pulled out my gloves and leather jacket and put them on. The stone was still there. There was no more use for a disguise. I took out the eye contacts and wiped the makeup off my face. My hair was knotted and nowhere near neat, but I pulled it back into a ponytail.

It was hard to wrap my head around the idea that I was working with Agent Watson now. We had spent so long fighting each other, arguing over events from the past. But now I would have to trust him. Or at least tolerate him.

As I closed my eyes, the conversation I heard from Ms. Blanchard's office came back to me. *I'm not sure if she has it. She doesn't know, but we could use her,* she had said.

116

Who was she even talking to? She said the T.S.O. wasn't meant to be public knowledge. It made my skin crawl. I couldn't get her words out of my head. Then there was the problem with Mr. O'Neil. He was working with someone in the organization. I couldn't help but think that the T.S.O. was in danger.

Chapter 30
When Rocks Glow

"Get up." I heard the words, but they didn't make sense. I opened my eyes to Damien shaking my arm.

"What?" My arm tightened around my bag. Working with Damien didn't mean he had to be in charge of the Bayshire. Or my sleeping schedule.

"The investor. He's here."

"Randall Bard is here?" I sat up in my seat, peeking over the seats.

"Not in this train car. But he's looking for you."

"If he's not in the car, then how do you know he's on the train?" I narrowed my eyes at him. Was this all a game to him?

"While you slept away, I actually did some work and checked out the whole train. I went to the other cars. He's on the one in front of us."

"Does he know who you are?"

"I don't think so."

This wasn't good. "Okay, so-"

"So, we keep our heads down and keep to ourselves." Damien interrupting me angered my sleepy brain.

I sighed heavily at Damien's interruption. *Keep it together. You're doing this for the T.S.O.* You're working together to reclaim your rank at base, to be a camp instructor and train new agents. He is helping you. He's a good guy. Put the past behind you.

"Let's start over," I said.

"Excuse me?"

"Let's start over. Let's forget about everything. The camp, the competitions. Let's start over." I put my hand out to shake, but my gesture didn't reach much further than that. "Hi. I'm Alexis."

Damien stared at me.

"Fine." I dropped my hand and crossed my arms. "But listen. If you want to work together, we need to act like partners. I can't stand your expressionless criticism every single second of my life." I looked him up and down, waiting for a response.

"You're acting unprofessional, Agent Mills. That's pathetic."

I lowered my voice even more. "Need I remind you we are out in public, trying to avoid attention. Stop calling me an agent."

"Alexis," he said, holding back his anger. "Understand that it was your idea we work together. If you don't want to, just give me the Bayshire and call it quits."

"Not a chance." I spit the words out.

"Suit yourself."

Turning away from Damien, I looked out the window. We were currently in Missouri. The lush clusters of trees filled the view outside my window. They whizzed past us in a blurry vision, my eyes struggling to find a single spot to focus on.

I pulled my headphones out of my bag, glimpsing at the stone. Its color shined from the reflection of the sun outside.

With my classic rock music in my ears and the sights outside, I fell into a steady beat of a four-count rhythm. With any luck, Mr. Bard wouldn't venture outside his train car.

Two more hours passed. We still had at least half a day left on the train. I took off my headphones, noting Watson ditched his seat next to me a while ago. At least he wasn't pestering me the entire trip. He was sitting behind me again, reading a book. Where he got it from, I had no idea. As far as I knew, Damien boarded without a single bag, not even the one he was carrying at the airport. Between the chairs I watched him, his eyes moving across the page.

I turned back around in my seat and stared at my bag. It was still very colorful, and I reached to change it back to its dormant black. But something stopped me. The duffle bag was getting warm against my legs.

I unzipped my bag. What I saw made my knees knock against each other, goosebumps spread across my arms. The Bayshire Stone was emitting a soft glow. And it was getting brighter.

Chapter 31
Mr. Bard Creates Smoke

My thoughts went back to the story in the Texas museum, the explosion that happened when the Bayshire was first being tested. The Bayshire was glowing, emanating heat right before everything went bad.

There were so many people on the train. So many innocent lives.

With my heart pounding and ready to jump out of my chest, I zipped up my bag. I whipped my head around. "Damien?"

The door at the front of the car burst open.

Mr. Bard rushed in. Even in his crazed state, his hair was still in perfect condition. He stormed down the aisle, inspecting everyone as he passed. What was I supposed to do? I wedged my bag between me and the wall. I looked behind me at Damien, who glanced between me and Mr. Bard.

He saw me. His nostrils flared and his eyes darkened. Mr. Bard marched over to me. I did my best to remain calm.

The Bayshire could mess up this whole train in a matter of minutes.

"The Bayshire Stone belongs to me," Mr. Bard growled. "You messed up everything."

Before I could respond, the lights on the ceiling flickered and faded all together.

Why was this happening? The stone wasn't exposed to anything! No one tried to mess with it, but it was still sending out electrical pulses.

"What's going on?" a woman in front of me asked. Her tone was layered with panic.

"Who turned off the lights?" said another. It was still daylight. Damien stood up behind me. What was he going to do? No. I couldn't let him do anything. I couldn't let the stone take down this train!

"Mr. Bard," I said, struggling to stay calm. "The Bayshire Stone is doing this."

Mr. Bard looked at my bag.

I saw what was in his hand. Mr. Bard clenched a device in his grip.

"What is that?" I asked, pointing to the device. It looked like a phone, but the shape was too square.

"This," he waved the device in front of my face and laughed. "This helped me find the stone. All the way from freaking California. This little device has constantly sent out electrical signals, receiving back energy from the surrounding magnetic fields, allowing me to track that stone. That stone that belongs to me and my company."

"Mr. Bard, you need to turn that thing off."

He reached for the bag. "I don't have to listen to anything you say."

I thrust a hand out to stop him. "That device of yours is messing with the stone. If it keeps sending out energy, the Bayshire is going to go off. It's already messed with the lights. It will take down this entire train!"

"Quit your lies! You're just a kid. Leave me alone and give me the stone. I won't press any charges. Otherwise, you'll be charged with everything you've done. And trust me, I know all about you and your secret organization. I've got some friends who might like that info."

What did he mean? Why wouldn't he listen to me? Across the aisle, a little kid's iPad flickered off. Mr. Bard grasped the bag and I clutched it tighter. He ripped the bag from my hands and stormed down the aisle. I didn't know what to say. He wasn't just threatening me. He was threating the entire organization. How did he even find out about the T.S.O.?

"I'm not lying!" I jumped out of my seat and grabbed the device from Mr. Bard's hand. He whirled around as every head in the car turned towards us. I shoved the device at Damien, who stood there waiting for something to happen. Mr. Bard wasn't leaving with the Bayshire Stone.

My duffel bag was smoking. We were too late.

Chapter 32
Stop the Train!

"Kid, sit down!" a man shouted at me. People were raising their voices. The train lurched forward, the brakes screaming. It didn't stop, but it slowed down. Was this the Bayshire's fault too?

Mr. Bard forgot about his tracking device. He reached to open the door, but it was thrust open before he could reach the handle.

"What's going on in here?" a man asked. He wore a waiter's uniform. He stepped into the train car.

"You have to stop the train!" I shouted. The man looked down at my bag in Mr. Bard's hands.

"Sir, I'm going to have to ask to see your bag."

I didn't want to cause any more panic. A little girl a few rows in front of me started crying. Too much was going on. There were kids on this train. I couldn't let them get hurt.

Someone put their hand on my shoulder. Damien whispered in my ear. "If we get the Bayshire far enough away from the train, it might stop disrupting the energy fields. The train would go back to normal and the Bayshire would die down once it's away from all the electricity."

That might work. The man in the doorway still blocked Mr. Bard, desperately asking him to stop shouting and explain himself.

I snatched the smoking bag, raced to the other end of the car, thrust open the door, and ran onto the balcony. There was a small set of stairs on the left. The sound of the train screeched on the tracks beneath me. I grabbed the rail as it lurched forward. My heart was racing and I couldn't keep up with it.

Through the open doorway, Mr. Bard tried to get past Damien. Damien wouldn't budge. I had to get off the train.

The straps of my bag got too hot to touch. I had no other choice.

With all my might, I threw the bag off the train. I jumped down the steps and rolled on my side into the grass.

The train kept going.

Sure, I had trained for things like this, but that didn't mean jumping off a moving train was painless. I pulled myself to my knees, groaning. I had scraped up my hands. My leg was screaming for me to lie down. The side of my head was throbbing. I begged for everything to stop aching. Ignore the pain. It wasn't important right now. There would probably be a few bruises by the next morning, but at least I was still in one piece. I might not have been prepared for moles in the organization, but at least the T.S.O. taught me some pain tolerance.

I got to my feet. Never in my lifetime did I imagine having to jump off a train. I limped a couple of steps forward and shook out the sore muscles in my legs. Looking down the tracks, I spotted my bag lying in the grass a ways off. I stumbled over to it, still finding my balance from the jump. I reached for my bag but jerked my hand back at its touch. It was still burning hot. Of course, the smoke coming from the zipper should have been my first clue.

Looking back at the train, a small blur jumped off the back before it disappeared down the tracks. I prayed it wasn't Mr. Bard and hoped it was only Agent Watson, something I would never have hoped for before.

"Great." I sighed. I still wasn't sure if he was a double agent, but I didn't believe he was. Either way, I was still stuck with him. I knelt beside my bag and forced the steaming zipper open. The zipper practically melted. The red glow was dying down. My headphones were ruined, and the Bayshire charred half my clothes. The bag's color-changing mechanism was fried. Wonderful. I slipped my arms out of my jacket and wrapped it around the straps of my bag. At least my jacket wasn't ruined. I slung my bag over my shoulder and started walking along the tracks.

"Nice of you to join me," I grumbled as I approached Damien. He wasn't in much better shape. The two of us started walking. "It was a good idea, getting the stone off the train."

Damien shrugged his shoulders. "What do we do now?"

"Just keep following the tracks until we come across a town, I guess. There has to be one soon. Then maybe we get on a bus the rest of the way." Again, I thought of getting my driver's license. Not that it would be of any use in the middle of nowhere, without a car. I glared at the never-ending tracks in front of me. "I'm done with trains."

"For once, we actually agree on something."

Chapter 33
Memories in the Middle of Nowhere

We walked for an hour. Then another. My shoulder ached from carrying the duffle bag. I unwrapped my jacket from around the strap and put it on. The bag was cool enough now.

"Want me to carry it?" Damien asked. I eyed him, wondering if it was some kind of trick. But he didn't have anywhere to go. I shrugged my shoulders and handed him my bag. Not a single train passed by. When I got bored, I walked on the tracks for a few minutes, zig-zagging across them, ignoring the tension in my leg. The pain was slowly going away, but it still hurt. Like Watson said, I had to work muscle into it, right?

"Why did you cheat?" Damien asked. It had been quiet for so long I jumped when he spoke? Was he seriously still upset about the competition? It was years ago.

"Why did you trip me at camp? Why does everything have to be a competition with you?" I asked, looking at him as I walked on the tracks.

"Fair enough."

"Besides, you already know the answer."

He sighed, shaking his head at me. "You make me so irritated, Alexis." There was tension in his voice as the words were spat out between his tightly shut teeth. He was holding back words.

"I never tried to make you irritated," I said, leaving the tracks and walking beside him. "I did my own thing with my friends and you thought I was out to get you or something."

"Ever since camp, it was always about you. You're so confident, it made me angry."

I scoffed at him. "My confidence made you angry?" I was not expecting this conversation.

"Yes."

I laughed. "Why?"

"I don't know," he said.

This conversation was getting awkward. I reached my hand out for the bag, and he handed it over without a single word. I readjusted the strap over my shoulder. There was nothing but trees and train tracks in sight. Everything was blurring together, and I began praying to God for a city to pop up.

"Is it wrong to be good at what I do?" I asked.

"No. But I'm good too. You just seem to steal the spotlight before I even get a chance to prove that." Damien was starting to sound insecure. It made me uncomfortable.

I said nothing. Did I really steal his spotlight? No wonder he hated me. Maybe I tried so hard because he always seemed more sure of himself, because Mr. Martial always liked him more. I would never admit that to him though. What were we supposed to talk about now? The Teen Spy Organization was how we met and our only form of a relationship. A crappy relationship at that.

I thought of telling him about the Director, about everything I overheard. But what if he was on the wrong side? What if he was a traitor like Mr. O'Neil? I mean, he had a good reason to not like the organization. I wanted to trust him so badly. I already blabbed my mouth off at the train station. I couldn't bring myself to say anything. As much as I didn't want to believe it, I was running low on people to trust.

"You think following the tracks is a safe idea?" Damien asked. I looked up at him. "The investor could have his men on us at any moment."

I nodded. It wasn't safe. I was getting hungry, and my throat was dry. "If we don't see anything in the next thirty minutes, we'll leave the tracks and head into the trees. Deal?" I asked.

"Deal."

We followed the tracks around a bend of trees, my feet pleading for me to stop. I opened my mouth to suggest we leave the tracks, when finally, there it was.

Civilization.

Chapter 34
Goodbye Headphones, Hello Snacks

A small town came up in front of us.

"Thank you, God!" I said as we walked into a gas station. I headed straight for the bathroom. I fixed my hair and ran some cold water over my face. At least the bag hadn't ripped, and it had stopped smoking.

The Bayshire Stone was back to its dormant state. All the better for me.

My feet ached from walking so far. My mind was tired of trying to make small talk with Damien. My confidence made him angry? That was an awkward thing to get mad at. Damien always seemed so confident, the way he carried himself, how he always had a snarky comment even when I didn't want them. Either way, it was time to focus on what I needed next. Food.

I bought a ready-made sandwich, some chips that I stashed in my bag for later, and three water bottles.

I downed an entire bottle and the sandwich on the walk to the bus station. I loved people. At the moment, the gas station could have been a five-star restaurant for all I cared. There were people around me and plenty of food. The three-hour walk wasn't bad, but trying to make conversation with a guy who hated you since the day you met was not a walk in the park.

Unfortunately, my headphones could not comfort me on the bus. They were broken, trashed, done for. I sighed as I threw them out. One of the earpieces was completely charred. The heat from the stone ruined the only thing in my bag I really cared about. They weren't worth saving. I would have to get a new pair once I got home. Which meant my long ride to Ohio was depressingly without music.

On the bus, I spent the entire ride watching the other travelers. Any one of them could be evil, working for Mr. Bard. By the time we made it to our next stop, the snacks in my bag were gone and I was down to half a bottle of water.

We stopped at a gas station to refuel. I followed Damien off the bus. After using the restroom, I bought another bottle of water and a protein bar. We didn't have much further to go. Every mile closer to home meant I was that much closer to finishing my mission.

Back outside, I waited with the group for the bus driver. The sun was preparing to set and exhaustion was calling my name. Damien didn't show up. People started boarding the bus. He was running out of time. Should I leave without him? He wasn't my responsibility. Besides, I had the Bayshire.

Not everybody was on the bus, but Watson should have been back. "Come on!" I groaned. Against my better judgment, I left my spot at the bus. As he said, any agent of the T.S.O. deserves help, right? I searched the entire gas station, but Damien wasn't there. I pulled down on my gloves and huffed out the door.

I walked around the building. There were three dumpsters and a few parked cars. There, in the middle of the parking lot, was Agent Watson.

He was kneeling on top of a large man, tying his hands with a rope behind his back. I watched from the edge of the building. Damien stood up, dusted off his hands, and turned away from the man. He must have been unconscious. His limbs were still, unmoving.

Damien spotted me and headed in my direction. "Did you worry about me?" he asked. "Come to watch the show?"

"Haha. The bus is ready to leave, and I didn't see you." I glanced at the unconscious man. He was on the bus with us. "Is that?" I nodded my head toward the unconscious man, my voice drifting as Mr. Bard's threat rang in my ears.

"One of Randall Bard's goons. Yeah. Didn't need him following us anymore."

"How did you know who he was?" I asked. Why didn't I spot him first on the bus?

Damien held a two-finger brass knuckle in his hand. I should have known. At least Damien caught him before anything bad happened. "He approached me in the men's room."

We started walking back to the group. I eyed the rest of the passengers, looking for the slightest hint they were out to get us.

"This investor guy has got people everywhere. We're not safe until we get back to base," I said.

"That's for sure." We got on the bus and took seats beside each other in the back. Damien was done talking. Did we actually just have a decent, agreeable conversation? The bus pulled out of the gas station and continued on to Cincinnati. What was happening?

Chapter 35
Welcome Home

My phone buzzed in my pocket. Damien eyed me as I answered it. It was Miles.

"Did you make the train?" he asked.

"Yes, Miles, I made the train."

"You should be here by now. What happened?"

I looked over at Damien. Miles wouldn't even believe me if I told him we were working together.

"I had some difficulty." Damien snorted. "I'll be back in about half an hour. Quit worrying."

"But you have the stone?"

"Yes. I have the stone." I thought of mentioning Ms. Blanchard, of overhearing her conversation. Better to talk in person. Phones could always be tapped.

"Just be careful," Miles said.

I hung up the phone before he could say anything else. I couldn't tell him about Ms. Blanchard. Something inside told me to keep the information to myself. I didn't know who I could trust. It was horrible, not knowing if I could trust my own friends. The thought left a sick feeling in my stomach. If the wrong people found out I knew something, even if I am just being paranoid, nothing good would come out of it.

"It was Miles, wondering where you were?" Damien asked.

"Yes," I said, shoving my phone in my pocket.

"He cares so much for you, Alexis." He drew out the words, making puppy dog eyes at me.

"Shut up!"

Damien didn't say anything else to me. He smiled to himself. I turned away from him.

The bus arrived in Cincinnati.

"Alright. We're here. I'll take the stone." Damien reached out his hand for my bag.

"Excuse me? No way!" I pulled away from him and turned down the street. "We take it in together. You agreed." I tensed. Was I wrong about him this time?

Damien didn't respond. He didn't attack or attempt to take the stone. His footsteps followed behind me down the pavement. His comment made me want to knee him in the gut. He was still trying to take all the credit. Part of me was impressed with his stubbornness. But no one was backing out of this sad partnership. Not yet.

With every step I took, my heart picked up speed. What was I going to say? And my parents. They had to know something was up by now. Who knew how long Tanner could keep my parents at bay?

With Damien following behind me, we arrived at the coffee shop. I sighed in relief. My night and day job all in one place. The coffee shop was busy as usual. Teens and young adults crowded into every booth. No one paid us any attention.

I walked up to the counter. Daniel was working the register. His eyes lit up.

"You're back!" he shouted. Did he even know where I went? Probably not. But it was nice to see one of my fans so excited at my return.

"And I brought a present." I smiled at him. He spotted Agent Watson behind me, eyes growing even wider. Everyone knew about our constant hate for each other, even the newbies.

I walked around the counter and into the back of the shop. Damien sighed behind me.

"What?"

"I wanted to be the one to walk in with the stone."

"Gee. So sorry you have to share it." I frowned at him sarcastically. Damien turned away from me and placed his hand on the scanner.

Together we walked into the small elevator, squeezing in. I clutched the bag tighter and held my breath. Why did the elevator have to be so small? Would it kill them to make it just a little bigger? I stared in front of me, waiting for the elevator to land.

This was the moment I was waiting for, to walk into the T.S.O. with my prize in hand, to reclaim the position I had, and wipe the past free of all shame. I know it sounded pathetic, but I didn't care. I had succeeded in my goal, and a bit more. I got the stone, helped some old friends, and made an alliance I never thought I would. Take that for leadership skills! I just hoped it would be enough, enough to prove I was still worthy of being Defense Tactics Instructor.

The door opened.

I followed Agent Watson out of the elevator and walked down the hall. We were going straight to Mr. Martial's office.

Young agents looked at me as I passed by. From what Damien said back at the Glayfield Museum about news traveling quickly, the looks I got weren't all welcoming.

How many rumors were there? I glanced at Damien, who smirked at me. And who started them?

I peeked into the training room, my favorite place in the base. It was empty. Tanner and Miles were probably around here somewhere, but they could wait.

I could hear my heartbeat thumping as we approached Mr. Martial's office. It was now or never.

"After you," Damien said, a fake smile revealing his pearly whites. I opened the door and stepped inside.

Chapter 36
Consequences

"Agent Mills!" Mr. Martial jumped out of his seat as he shouted my name. I pulled down on my gloves and held on tighter to the duffel bag.

"Sir."

"Agent Watson, explain." Mr. Martial's dark brown eyes never left my face. He was angry, and he wanted me to know it.

"Mr. Martial, I went after the Bayshire Stone as directed," Damien started. "At the Glayfield Museum, I ran into Agent Mills." He was so formal I wanted to punch him. His hands folded behind his back, his straight posture and annoying haircut rubbing it in. But he didn't mention following me at the airport. Or that I got the stone first. Hmm.

Mr. Martial glared at me harder. "Agent Mills, I hope you know the consequences of disobeying a direct order from your superiors."

I bit the inside of my cheek. "With all due respect Sir, I believe I was wrongfully removed from the case and therefore made my own decision to continue it on my own. I understand fully the consequences I may have to endure." Mr. Martial opened his mouth to speak. "But I would like to inform you that my rogue mission was successful. And if it wasn't for Agent Watson assisting me, we would have lost the stone and it would have caused major damage."

Mr. Martial turned towards Damien. "And what about you?"

"She is correct, Sir."

I stepped up to Mr. Martial's desk. With a deep breath, I pulled out the Bayshire Stone from my bag and placed it on the table in front of him.

Mr. Martial's gaping mouth and rare silence were priceless. "Agent Mills, I'm impressed," he started after he got over his shock at me actually getting the stone. I impressed him? That was a first. "Although your disobeying orders is *not* acceptable, it is good to see you don't give up." Mr. Martial sat down. He looked up at me with an expression I hadn't seen before. I had never impressed him before. "Maybe I was wrong. Clearly you were more capable of pursuing your case than I expected. Well done."

Did I just get a compliment? I nodded my head, resisting the urge to smile. He gave me a compliment!

"If I may, Sir…" Mr. Martial nodded at me. "Mr. Bard is still a danger. He pursued us on our way back from California. He's still looking for the stone." His threat on the train flashed in my head.

"We have been keeping tabs on him. No one had spotted him entering the state yet." Mr. Martial sat back down. "Agent Mills, you deliberately disobeyed my orders and involved other agents of the T.S.O. This can't go overlooked."

I nodded, swallowing down my fear. Couldn't he just go back to being impressed by me? Mr. Martial opened his mouth to speak. I held my breath, hoping this wasn't the end of the road for me.

"I'll have to take this up with the other directors. You're dismissed."

Chapter 37
When I Cause Difficulties

I was confused. "Is that it?"

"Yes. I will have to talk to the Board of Directors. Even though you retrieved the Bayshire, you must be held accountable for your disobeying orders, Agent Mills. Do you understand?" Mr. Martial looked at me, and for a moment I thought there was a hint of irritation. Irritation that wasn't directed towards me.

"Yes, Sir."

"Agent Watson," Mr. Martial said, directing his attention to Damien. Damien stood up straighter and stuck out his chest. So, mister big shot was nervous. "I understand that retrieving the Bayshire was your case." Mr. Martial glared at me for a second. I kept myself from sighing. "I have my own issues with Agent Mills, and I'm sorry if she caused any difficulties, but at least the job was accomplished."

Now I was mad. Difficulties? Clearly Mr. Martial wasn't in his right mind.

"Please deliver the Bayshire Stone to the safety facility and make sure it's locked up tight."

"Yes, Sir."

Damien grabbed the stone from Mr. Martial's desk and left his office.

"Agent Mills." Mr. Martial eyed me. My face felt hot. "According to T.S.O. standards, I do have to suspend you." I gave a slight nod. I should have seen this coming. It wasn't likely that I would have been completely off the hook. "Because you finished the job without casualties, I will not remove you from your position. But I am giving you a three weeks suspension."

"I understand, Sir."

I was too afraid to ask about being the Defense Tactics Instructor. If I had any luck left, in three weeks I might be able to continue my job as it were. My face was burning with embarrassment. But I did the right thing, didn't I? Damien wouldn't have been able to get it on his own. Even I had help from my friends.

"You're dismissed," Mr. Martial said.

For once, I was quiet.

I stepped out of his office and stared at my shoes.

"That bad?" I looked up and faced Damien. He was still standing in the hall, holding the Bayshire Stone. The crazy rock that might have caused me to ruin my career.

"Sorry if I caused any *difficulties*," I said, drawing air quotes around the word.

"Although you are an immense irritation, I don't know why he made that comment," Damien said. "What did he give you?"

I rolled my eyes and stared at the wall. "Three weeks suspension. I deserved it." Damien didn't smile, didn't make a single comment about my punishment. Instead, he nodded. He probably agreed, though. I deserved it.

"Look, I've got to get this to the safety facility," he said. "And you probably have people waiting for you somewhere."

141

I nodded. Damien was right. The thought left a foul taste in my mouth.

"Let's get one thing straight," he said. I waited for him to continue. "We are not friends. We never were."

"Agreed."

"Good." Agent Watson turned and walked away from me.

"Good," I repeated. I held on tighter to my bag and headed the opposite way. Not friends. But I could trust him. I was sure of it.

Then it hit me. Mr. Martial said he was impressed with me. Yes, he punished me, but I impressed him. I let myself smile as I walked down the hall. My mission wasn't pointless. If anything, I gained at least a little respect from my director. That was something worth cherishing!

Before leaving the base, I had to find Tanner and Miles. I guess I was avoiding seeing my parents as long as possible. I knew they would be furious. But I had to find my friends. My breath caught in my throat at the thought of seeing Tanner. I had never done a case without a partner. Of course, technically I still hadn't.

I searched the entire base. Miles was nowhere to be found. I headed towards the access point to the café. I was not looking forward to when I got home. I turned the corner into the office area. Tanner walked out of the access point to the café. His boot was gone, along with the crutches. I smiled. Was I blushing? I sure hoped not.

"What did Mr. Martial say?" he asked. Straight to the point.

"Well, I'm in trouble."

Tanner nodded. There was a tug at his lips.

"I think everything will be okay. Hopefully. By the way, congrats on getting rid of the boot," I said, nodding at his foot.

"Thanks." Tanner blushed. I opened my mouth to say something, but he cut me off. "You were gone too long."

Now it was my turn to blush. "Really?" What exactly did that mean?

Tanner shrugged his shoulders. "Maybe a little." I wanted to say something, but I couldn't think of anything. "I mean, I've been trying to keep your parents calm, but I've just about run out of options. I've been telling them that the school trip was extended, that your flights had to get rebooked, that those ones were delayed. I suggest you get home soon. Last thing they knew, your flight from Texas was canceled and your group had to take a train instead."

"Thanks, Tanner."

Tanner nodded and then smiled. An actual smile you could see. "See you, partner."

"See you." I gave a nod and stepped into the elevator before things could get any more awkward. What just happened? I couldn't keep my ears from burning. Why couldn't I stop smiling? I rushed out of the café before Daniel could ask me any questions.

When I arrived home, the thought of sleep almost felt comforting. I walked up the steps to my front porch. I was a disaster. I was still wearing the same clothes as the day before, and half my outfits were burned to a crisp inside my bag. My hair was a mess, as usual, and I was covered in scrapes and bruises I wasn't ready to explain.

Mom and Dad would be outraged!. Did they even know I was back in the state? Where did they think I was, considering everything Tanner kept telling them? My body ached wondering if they thought something bad happened to me. I sighed. As long as they knew I was safe, everything would turn out okay.

I pulled my house key out of my bag.

Chapter 38
I Was on a Case

"Where, on God's green earth, have you been!?" shouted Dad as he jerked the door open, almost pulling it off its hinges before I even inserted the key.

Mom pushed Dad aside and pulled me into her arms as tight as possible. "We were so worried!" She let go of me and shoved me inside. There were tears running down her cheeks and dark circles under her eyes. I felt so awful I didn't even cringe as Mom looked me over and pulled me into a hug tight enough to crack a rib.

Dad stood in front of me. "You have some explaining to do." I let my bag fall to the ground. So much for his "once in a lifetime opportunity" attitude.

Mom and Dad bombarded me with questions. "Where have you been?" "Why were you gone so long?" "What happened?" "Why didn't you call us?" And they kept coming. I looked back and forth between them, my head about to fly through the roof. I couldn't take the questions all at once. I knew what they were thinking. They were thinking about Hailey and having possibly lost me too. Guilt washed over me like a tsunami. How could I have done this to them?

"Okay!" I shouted, taking a step back from them. They stared at me, waiting for answers. Lies weren't going to cut it. Not this time. I took a deep breath, preparing myself for what came next. My parents waited expectantly, hands on hips, jaws clenched.

"I was on a case, and it didn't go so well," I said.

"Cut it out, Alexis, what happened?" Dad asked.

"I was on a case," I said again, holding back tears myself.

"What do you mean, a case?" asked Mom.

"The whole trip was a fake!" I flung my arms out to my sides.

Now they were silent, eyes wide as they looked back and forth from me to each other, again and again.

"I knew it!" Mom shouted, pointing a finger in my face. "Prepaid, fully funded, whatever. Tanner and his…his extended trip nonsense. I knew something else was going on." Her face was red from crying, and her smile looked out of place.

"Alexis, what on earth were you thinking? Where did you go?" Dad demanded an answer.

"I'll explain once you stop yelling!"

Yep, I was grounded. I let out a long breath of air, trying to think about what to say. Might as well tell them everything. Almost everything.

"I've been working for an undercover agency and I had to leave the state to carry out a mission." If I told them I did that without permission, well, I was already dead.

"Undercover agency? Did you even go to Texas? What are talking about?" Dad shouted. Mom looked ready to cry again.

"I work for an agency called the Teen Spy Organization." No sign of recognition crossed their faces. "I'm a spy," I said.

"Enough with the lies, Alexis," Dad huffed.

145

"I'm not lying! Do you remember that camp I went to a few years ago?" Mom nodded her head. She was beginning to understand. "That was the start of it. That was the first level of training."

"So, you've been a part of a secret spy agency run by teenagers for three years?" Mom's voice shook, her eyes glossy. She made it sound absurd, impossible. I nodded. Dad stared at me. He still didn't believe me. I knelt down and unzipped my bag, digging around in the mess of ruined clothes until I found my badge.

"Here. Proof."

Dad took the badge from me, in its belt strap and all. I had memorized what it looked like. Agent Mills was written on the top of the silver circle. Teen Spy Organization engraved on the bottom. T.S.O. etched into the middle of the design.

"You're telling me you're a spy, and you tricked us to fly out of state for a job?" Dad looked completely beside himself.

"Yes." I took the badge back and squeezed it in my hands.

"Why?" they said at the same time.

"I had to…to get something from Texas. But it took longer than expected. That's why I was gone for so long." Again, they were silent. I held my breath, my stomach churning. The moment lasted forever.

Mom stepped forward and wrapped her arms around me. Usually she was the one that got mad at me first.

"Why are you doing this?" Dad asked. Mom let go of me.

I was shaking now. And despite my attempts to prevent it, tears started to fall down my cheeks. I wiped them away and stood up straighter. "Because I keep other people from getting hurt. You can't keep me from doing this," I said." I turned to Mom and forced the tears to go away. *Get*

146

it together. She understood. Mom smiled, but her sadness wasn't hard to see.

"You stink," she said, holding me at arm's length. Her voice was shaking. "Go take a shower. We'll talk about this after you freshen up."

I slung my bag over my shoulder and walked further into the house. I could feel Dad's eyes, sharp and cold, glaring into the back of my head as I walked into my room.

As soon as I got out of the shower, all hell was going to break loose.

Chapter 39
Grounded

There was a knock on my bedroom door. I stuffed my charred clothes into the closet and kicked the door shut with my foot as the bedroom door opened.

Mom and Dad both walked in. Neither of them were smiling. I honestly never thought this day would come, that they would find out about the T.S.O., but it was too late to go back. If Mr. Martial was a cartoon character, steam would come out of his ears once he heard about this.

There were a few agents who had parents that knew about the T.S.O. Most didn't though, and it was designed that way to keep the T.S.O. as secret as possible and protect their agents' identities.

"I'm sorry that I lied," I said. I stood in front of them with my damp hair around my face and my eyes red from crying in the shower. After everything I went through, my parents were my biggest obstacle. I was glad they cared so much. "I understand that I'm in trouble," I said.

"Phone," Dad demanded, hand outreached and waiting. I picked up my phone from my bed and placed it in his palm.

"Ground me, take away the computer, whatever."

"You're not allowed to leave the house, do you understand?" Dad asked. His voice was crisp, firm. I didn't like the sound of it.

"I understand." Besides, it wasn't like my schedule was busy at work for the next three weeks.

"And you have to wait until the fall to start Driver's Ed." Dad knew where to hurt me, but I guess I deserved it.

"I just don't understand why you didn't tell us," Mom said.

"You wouldn't have let me do it." Mom nodded, knowing I was right. After Hailey died, there was no way she would have let me join the T.S.O. if she had known about it. "I'm doing good in the world and it's important," I said.

"Three weeks of punishment," Dad said. "Then, with our permission, I guess you could continue working for this...agency. It sounds like you're doing some sort of good. But I want to meet these people."

Was he serious? I hadn't expected him to let me continue. Maybe they did actually understand, at least a little.

"Thank you!" I shouted, wrapping my arms around him. I felt his muscles relax. I stepped away and Dad turned and left my room. He was still mad, but he understood how important it was to me. He and Mom must have talked the whole time I was in the shower.

Mom didn't move. She didn't speak. Mom stared at me, ready to fall apart or start yelling. It was hard to tell which one.

"I'm sorry," I whispered, bowing my head.

"Why didn't you tell me?" she asked again.

149

"You would say being a spy is too dangerous. After what happened to Hailey-"

"I would," she said, cutting me off. Neither of us said anything. Mom looked away from me, her eyes browsing the various photos on my wall. "I need you to understand something." She met my eyes, and I waited for her to continue. "I'm angry you lied, you kept secrets. You scared me. But I'm proud you've become responsible enough to tell the truth and to know how to handle yourself. Hailey would be proud too. Please, just don't lie to me anymore."

"I won't, Mom. I promise."

Chapter 40
Free to Go

Since it was summer, and school was out, there was no leaving the house. Period. There were no phone calls with friends. I still hadn't talked to Miles or Sarah.

I spent my time watching movies with Mom and playing card games. It wasn't so bad. I went to bed with Mr. Bard's threat hanging in the air. He knew about the T.S.O. How? What was he going to do? He didn't just give me an empty threat. He meant every word. He was still going to be a problem, my problem. During the day, I felt safe. I was home, back in my bed, with food on the table. At least I wasn't jumping off any more trains or being followed. Hopefully.

Mom wasn't as mad at me anymore. Neither was Dad. Although, I definitely lost his trust. For now. I felt guilty all over again every time he looked at me. He couldn't look me in the eye. With any luck, that would change soon.

I thought of Amelia, Agent Z. Did her parents know about her accident? They had to. They had to know something. Of course, her parents were probably lied to like mine were. That's the one problem with the T.S.O. They encourage agents to lie. To make up stories. Sometimes that just leads to bigger problems.

Then finally, my three weeks had passed! My time being grounded and suspended had come to an end.

"You're free," Dad said, handing me back my phone. "Remember, we have to know what you're doing and where you are at all times. Understood?"

"Understood." I smiled, pulling my arm through my leather jacket. "I'll be at work."

"And where is that exactly?"

"The same coffee shop I've worked at for the past year."

Dad nodded. Mom smiled behind him. I had told her the T.S.O. was located underground, the café was my way in. Dad would understand better coming from her.

When the elevator landed in the T.S.O. Base, my skin was tingling with excitement and dread.

Chapter 41
Camp Preparations

I checked in at the desk to verify I was back in action. I wanted to go to the gym, finally find Miles and have a proper combat session and make up for all the time I'd been gone.

"Agent Mills!" The woman at the check in desk exclaimed. "Welcome back!"

"Thanks." I tugged on my gloves and smiled.

"Mr. Martial is waiting for you. He's in his office."

As I headed through the halls, people were running everywhere. There were more agents in the base at once than usual. Training camp. A banner was posted on the wall in the cafeteria. My heart skipped a beat.

I knocked on Mr. Martial's door. "Sir?" I asked, stepping into his office.

"Agent Mills. I was starting to think you were gone for good."

"Only in your dreams, Sir."

"Hmm." I stood up straighter, grasping my hands behind my back. Mr. Martial put down his pen and straightened a pile of papers on his desk. I shifted my weight, trying to hold my tongue. This was either really good, or really bad.

"Agent Mills, you have been officially reinstated as Defense Tactics Instructor at the T.S.O. Training Camp this summer."

My jaw dropped. It was what I've been waiting to hear! Until he actually said it, part of me thought I would never get to be an instructor. I could hardly believe it, I almost wanted to hug Mr. Martial. Almost. "Camp begins in less than a month," he said.

"Yes, Mr. Martial."

The Director looked less than happy. "The Board of Directors decided even though you *disobeyed* orders and left the state without permission to continue a case that was given to *someone else*, your actions showed your determination and dedication to the agency." I couldn't help but smile at this point. "The Board of Directors agreed that they will excuse your past actions in the field, for now. You've served your punishment. Your performance in the field and reports from agents who have shadowed you in the field have shown the directors you're still fit for the job."

"Thank you, Sir." I thought of Ms. Blanchard, whose opinion on the Board of Directors was always important, especially when it came to the camp. She had let me continue my mission. And she had a reason for it.

"I would disagree with your actions in disobeying my direct orders, but I guess they're right," Mr. Martial grumbled. Was that actually a compliment? I wasn't sure, but I would take it as one. "They want you there."

"I wouldn't miss it for the world, Sir." Images of my fall from the rock wall flashed through my mind, something Mom and Dad still knew nothing about. A moment of panic welled up inside me, but I replaced it by thinking about all of the amazing memories at camp with my friends. It was going to be a fun summer!

"Dismissed."

I left his office, ready to shout. To go back to the place where the T.S.O. first became a possibility in my life made my head spin with excitement. To go back to California, to teach new agents. This was what I actually wanted, and I got it! I had to find Tanner and Miles. I had to thank Miles for all of his help. After all, I might never have successfully pursued the Bayshire Stone without him.

Chapter 42
Miles

I texted Tanner, and we agreed to meet later. My stomach fluttered at the thought of it. Now I just had to find Miles, who wasn't answering his phone. I entered the gym, but Miles wasn't there. He wasn't in the office area or the cafeteria either. He probably wasn't here.

I walked through the halls and pulled out my phone to call Miles again. Why wasn't he answering?

There were voices up ahead. No, only one voice.

I stopped before turning the corner. After listening to Ms. Blanchard's private conversation, I wasn't going to take any chances.

It was Miles. I tucked my phone in my pocket. "Yes," Miles said, in the most serious tone I had ever heard from him. I risked it and poked my head around the corner. Miles had his phone up to his ear, facing away from me. I stepped back around the corner and leaned as close to the icy wall as I could.

Miles started talking again. "I think I can persuade her." Who was he talking about? I was ready to walk up to him when he answered whoever was on the other end. "Yes, Sir. The Bayshire Stone is here. I checked myself." The Bayshire Stone, the thing I risked my entire career for. There was a pause. "No, she'll be going to camp." The person on the other line must have been angry because Miles sighed. "But, Sir, it might work to our benefit. People trust her. People who don't know her trust her. With Agent Mills being an enormous influence on new kids at camp, we might have more people on our side when the time comes. And if not, she will be out of the way."

He was talking about me. Why was he talking about me?

"Well, when it's time, we'll need that type of person on our side." Who was he talking to? "I'm aware of what the Director thinks." There was a pause. "I'm aware of that too. But we have more people on our side now."

I started focusing on my breathing. I had to stay quiet. This wasn't good.

"Don't worry. I'll get Agent Mills. One way or another."

Miles' voice stopped. I listened to his footsteps quiet as he walked down the hall. I pushed all my weight against the wall and struggled to slow my breathing with little success. Everything that I had learned, that I had seen. Mr. O'Neil in the prison, a traitor working inside the T.S.O., Amelia and Emily's suspicions of Ms. Blanchard. The Director's odd questions and conversations. And there were Mr. Bard's men, always knowing where I was, the woman at the coffee shop in Texas, the man at the gas station with Damien. People had been watching me this entire time. I was still being watched. But who was watching me?

As soon as Miles' footsteps faded, I ran in the opposite direction down the hall. I had to find Damien. After everything we had been through, I knew I could trust him. But Miles? He was my friend. I never would have questioned him! Maybe I should have. He planned my trip, knew my every location, except when I was on the bus, when he called me. What was he up to? I had to find Tanner. Did he know about any of this? I prayed that I could still trust him. I spun around the corner and forced myself to run faster, farther away from Miles.

Damien and Tanner, I had to tell them. I had to find them before Miles could do anything. Miles could not be trusted. The T.S.O. was in trouble, somehow. My mission wasn't over yet.

Continue the adventure in *Recruited*.

Have you read the first book in the T.S.O. series yet?

T.S.O. Finding Doom

Check it out on Amazon.

Learn more at reklinzing.com

Acknowledgements

This book has been a part of a very big journey for me. Publishing my second book feels like a leap further in my career as an author. I would never have made it without all the amazing help and support from my friends and family during this crazy time. First, I want to thank the Lord for giving me the passion to write. Without God this story would never have happened.

A lot of people went into the making of this story, and it's only fitting to mention them and how much they contributed. I want to thank Chelsea Fuchs, who is such an amazing editor. Without her incite and guidance, this story wouldn't be what it is. I also want to thank all of my beta readers. I know we didn't get everything done this time the way we planned, but your help and support mean so much to me.

I want to thank my parents. I know we went through a lot during the making of this book, but you didn't give up on me. And Mom, you are an amazing editor. You mean more to me than words can express. I just want to make sure you know that. Without your help, I would never have made it this far.

I thank all of my siblings for their love and support. I know I'm not always easy to deal with. Audrey, you carried me through my worst times while working on this story. You sat and listened to me ramble off plot ideas and bounce every silly thought I had off you, but you never pushed me away. We wouldn't have the love interest in this story if it wasn't for you. You laughed at my silly story ideas and talked about the characters as if they lived next door, even though you haven't read the whole story yet. You really are my wall, offering support and standing strong when I need you the most. Alexis means so much to me because she reminds me of you. That's why this story is dedicated to such an amazing sister, my "Partner in Crime."

Well, last but definitely not least, I thank all my amazing readers. You are the ones who bring this story to life, who make the words fly off the page every time you open the book and jump into the world of the T.S.O. Without you this story wouldn't live beyond my imagination. You're so awesome!

About the Author

R.E. Klinzing lives with her family in Southern California. Aside from writing, R.E. Klinzing is studying to be an ASL Interpreter. When she isn't writing, she spends her time reading, enjoying outdoor activities, and watching way too many crime shows with her sister. R.E. Klinzing's goal is to inspire young writers to pursue their dreams and ignite a love of reading within every person that opens a book.

Join the newsletter for special updates and learn more at reklinzing.com!